The story, all names, characters, and incidents portrayed in this production are fictitious. No identification with actual persons (living or deceased) is intended or should be inferred.

Copyright © 2025 by M.P. Hendy

All rights reserved

No part of this publication may be reproduced, distributed, or transmitted in any form or by any means, including photocopying, recording, or other electronic or mechanical methods, without the prior written permission of the publisher, except as permitted by U.S. copyright law.

First paperback edition: April 2025

Book cover by Perchance AI Generator

ISBN   978-1-9680272-9-2 (5x8 paperback)

The Survivor's Regression

Part II

David's Chosen Family

M.P. Hendy

Table of Contents

Chapter 15

Heartbreaking News

Summer was finishing her shift at the clinic as she was approached by her supervisor, "We've got more people coming in, this time it's a woman's husband, he suddenly collapsed in his home, and they think it's a heart attack." She shook her head, "Look, I know it's been really busy, but I've been on call for the past sixteen hours and if I don't get a shower and take a nap, I'm going to be next." As he sighed, she turned to leave. He knew he couldn't stop her, but the hospitals were full, and neighboring clinics were forced to pick up the slack.

As she tried to start the car, the push button ignition was unresponsive. After several tries, she eventually resorted to using the metal key within the key fob. "Finally!" she said excitedly. As she drove home, she tried to turn on the radio, but none of the entertainment systems worked, not even the navigation. Frustrated at the situation, she reflected on the day. She was on rotation at the emergency clinic for the weekend and this weekend was supposed to be a breeze.

Her shift started at 8:00pm and she was only supposed to work until 8:00am, but it was after lunch and the only thing she had eaten was the chocolate teddy bear her husband bought her for Valentine's day. It wasn't until after midnight that the night got hectic; first a blackout shut everything off, including the phones. Thankfully, their emergency generators came on, however, that did nothing to fix the internet. Even some people's cellphones stopped working. Even though the clinic had backup power, most places still had no electricity, and the networks were still down. It wasn't until around 5:00am that the clinic started to get crowded. First it was the elderly, then random people showed up.

As she pulled into her driveway, she was frustrated to see that her power was off. Her husband was at work already and dishes were in the sink, but otherwise the house was clean, after all, no one was ever home long enough to leave a mess. Leaving her purse on the kitchen counter, she immediately took a shower, desperate to finally get some sleep. Twenty minutes later, she finally came out of her room, wearing pajama pants and an oversized t-shirt. As she sat on the couch, she poured a glass of rum and coke, something that always made her sleepy.

Suddenly she was woken up by the door slamming, her husband had rushed home, locking the doors and peeking through holes in the window. Freaking out by his aggressive movements, "What the hell is going on out there?" "Just stay in the house!" he demanded. His clothes were disheveled, and the house smelled like garbage and waste, making her nauseous. Running to the bathroom to wash her face, she was shocked at the person in the mirror, her hair was out of sorts and her skin was flush. As she reached for a water bottle to rinse her face, the sight of her toilet nearly made her throw up. She poured water into her hand and rubbed her face, drying off with her shirt before walking out.

As she entered the living room, she was shocked to see two strangers sleeping on the couch. When did they get there?

Where was her husband? The house reeked of body odor and urine, making it difficult to breathe. As she walked through the house looking for her husband, she went into the garage. "My car is missing!" she exclaimed. Turning back to her room, she was stopped by one of the men sleeping on the couch. "You're a woman, why don't you get me something to eat," he demanded. Summer shook her body free before responding, "Get the fuck off of me!" Walking into the bedroom, she heard her husband in the bathroom, as she turned, she saw him standing in his underwear while pissing in a water bottle. "It's so fucking hot!" he said in an exhausted tone. As he set the bottle next to the sink, she could feel her stomach turning in disgust.

As she turned to leave the bathroom, a hand grabbed her arm. Turning around, she recognized the man from earlier as he slapped her, knocking her to the ground. "Let me go! Help me!" she screamed for help, but nobody came. Suddenly, two arms grabbed her from behind, pulling her to the couch as she struggled to break free. The man before her smiled with a sickly face, exposing his yellow teeth, wearing nothing but a pair of old basketball shorts. She continued to kick her feet, hoping to break free. Just then she heard her husband's voice in her ear. "Now now, don't worry. It's going to be okay." A kiss pressed against the side of her cheek as she closed her eyes.

As if snapping out of a trance, she opened her eyes. The man was pulling off her shorts as the arms that held her down gripped tighter. Tears began to run down her cheeks as her husband's voice floated into her ears, "Don't fight him dear, I promise this will be over soon." Like a slap in the face, reality came crashing down as the man pulled down his shorts while her husband held her down. In that moment, Summer screamed, begging for a miracle, anything to deliver her from this moment. As she closed her eyes, the smell of his breath burned her lungs as she gagged.

"Summer! Wake up, or we're going to be late!" a young woman screamed as she put on her shoes. Summer sat up in her bed, carefully looking at her surroundings. Still disoriented, she put her shoes on and rushed to follow the other woman out the door. With minutes to spare she rushed to take her seat. "Today's lesson is on unconventional pharmaceuticals!" Summer lowered her head as the professor continued the lecture. Her head was still spinning from this morning and the only thing she could think about was David. What was he doing now? Did I have that dream because of him? She couldn't concentrate on anything. It had been nearly two and a half years since she saw him, and she was beginning to doubt if she had made the right decision. Internships would be starting in the fall, and she wanted to see him before then. As the class continued, she took out her notebook and began writing down the details from her dream, a smile growing on her face. It seems that his habits have rubbed off on her.

Two weeks later, school was starting the summer term, and she decided to take that time off. On the way home, she stopped at a travel agency to look at flights, but on short notice, everything was expensive, especially this time of year. "What if he's moved on?" Shaking off her thoughts, she purchased a round trip ticket. "Even if he did, I still need to find out," she mumbled. After arriving at her father's house, she called her reserve liaison to tell him of her travel plans. Surprisingly, he agreed to contact the military hospital at her destination so she could serve her time there for the month, something she wasn't expecting.

With renewed excitement, she quickly packed her bags, making sure to include her uniform and boots. The next morning, her father drove her to the airport, unaware of her ulterior motives. "Have a good time at drill sweetheart, call me if you have any trouble." She hugged him as she left the car, dragging her carry-on bag with her through the terminal. After checking in, she went through security, then sat in the terminal, waiting for her flight. She had gotten to the airport with plenty of time to spare, excited for her trip, so she decided to buy a coffee, something she never thought she would do, until it suddenly became necessary.

According to her boarding pass, her flight would be landing at 2:40pm. Hopefully she'll make it before it gets too late. On the plane, she spent the entire flight writing in her book, making her own plans as if everything David told her was certain. She was required to complete her reserve contract, which she was committed to for at least another three years, but what if she could change her reserve unit? Then she would have to stay in an unfamiliar place for at least six months when David left again, and what about college? What if she got pregnant? "Shut up Summer," she mumbled.

As the plane landed, her heart began to pound, doubt and apprehension began to fog up her thoughts. What if he's already married? He did say he was married before, maybe he did it again? As she left the terminal, she looked for a pay phone, pulling a slip of paper from her pocket. "Hello?" "Hello Sergeant Barker?" she responded. "Yes, this is he." "This is Specialist Bellerose, I was told to give you a call when I got in." "Yes, Specialist Bellerose, your Sergeant called and said you would be in town this month. We won't need you until next week, but why are you calling me now? Don't you have a place to stay?" he asked concerned. "That's just it, I do, but I don't know where he lives and I was hoping you could help," she asked nervously. "Sure, I'll come pick you up. Do you at least know what unit he's in?" he asked. "Yes, yes I do." "Good, sit tight, I should be there in about an hour." Summer hung up the phone, sighing deeply. It was already 3:15pm, so if it takes him an hour, I might not get there until this evening.

Nearly an hour later, a blue pickup truck pulled in front of her, driven by a tall black Soldier wearing BDUs. "Is this all you brought?" he asked. "Yes, I packed light this time," she smiled. After putting her bag in the back of the truck, they headed toward the base. "So, what's it like here?" she asked. "It's humid as fuck," he responded sarcastically. "So, what do you do when you aren't drilling?" he asked. "I'm in a program trying to get my Doctor of Pharmacy degree, but I don't know anymore. We're on summer break for now. I originally wanted to be a nurse practitioner, but that's a lot of school and something changed my mind," she said hesitantly. "Something or someone?" he asked curiously.

As they pulled up to the Battalion headquarters, she looked at her watch. "I thought it would take an hour?" He smiled, "No, but it takes me half an hour to get out of work." She waved as he left, carrying her bag. As she walked up to the front door, several people passed, holding the door for her. "Hello, can

I help you?" the staff duty officer asked. "Yes, I just arrived and I'm looking for someone, he doesn't know I'm here," she responded. "Are you a family member or a service member?" he asked. "No and yes, here's my ID card. I'm here on drill," she said, holding out her military ID. "Who is it you're here to see?" "David Renado," she answered. "Let me make a phone call real quick," he said as he picked up the phone. "Yes, this is Sergeant Nelson at the Battalion Staff Duty, there's a Specialist Summer Bellerose here for Sergeant Renado. Yes. I don't know. Sure, Okay." After hanging up the phone, he handed back her ID card and gave her directions to the Battalion Dining Facility.

The walk was longer than she thought. As she stood in front of the building, outside the main door, several Soldiers told her how to get to the main entrance. Upon her arrival, she stood in an empty dining room, looking for a familiar face. Just then a tall Staff Sergeant called out to her. "Are you Bellerose?" "Yes Sergeant!" she responded instinctively. "Don't worry about that kind of shit here, besides, you aren't active, are you?" "No Sergeant." As he gestured to an empty seat, he sat across from her. "Sergeant Renado is already off today, but I don't know you and before I call him, I want to make sure you aren't here to cause any trouble," he said seriously. "I understand completely," she responded respectfully.

"What is your relationship to David Renado?" he asked. She thought before answering, "I was his classmate in high school, plus, we're friends." He thought for a moment before asking his next question. "What's your relationship to his wife?" Her heart sank while trying to find an answer, "His wife? When I knew him, he didn't have a wife," she said, reaching up to hold her neck. "But if I did, I would hope we were friends." He sat back for a moment before standing up. "Okay, I'll call him in, but I don't want to be responsible for starting a problem." She nodded her head, trying to hold in her tears as he went to make the call. "Okay, I just called him, he should be here in about fifteen minutes, if you want, you can wait here and have something to drink, but don't touch the food." She nodded, standing up to get a cup of juice.

After finishing her juice, she noticed a familiar figure passing in the corner of her eye, walking straight to the office. As she waited, she secretly hoped the world would swallow her up before he saw her. Stepping out of the office, he instantly made eye contact with her. Summer's eyes began to fill with tears as she stared at him, seemingly unphased by her presence. "Come here Summer," he commanded in a stern tone. As she stood, she slowly approached, hands clenched in front of her, looking toward the ground. Standing in front of him, she was afraid to move and even more afraid to speak. "Where is your collar?" he asked. At that moment, it was like a dam broke. She grabbed him tightly, crying as she hung onto his neck, "It's in my bag," she whimpered. "Then go and get it," he ordered with a smile on his face.

Running to her bag, she quickly pulled the sterling chain from the top pocket and ran to hand it to him. "Turn around," he commanded. Without hesitation, she turned around and lifted her hair as he wrapped the chain around her neck. When she turned back around, she kissed him hard on the lips, creating a look of panic and confusion on the staff sergeant's face. Summer grabbed her bag and the two of them immediately got into his car. David started the car, and she looked at him with a serious expression, "So, I heard you're fucking married!"

David didn't respond but began driving. After several minutes, he pulled into a parking space in front of a large building. David's house was a quad, and the parking spaces were communal. Grabbing her bag from his trunk, he walked toward the front door. Summer's heart raced as she scanned the area, looking for any sign of activity. "Don't look too hard, military dependents tend to be quite nosey, and we don't need that kind of attention." Nodding her head, she quietly followed him inside the house. Everything was clean, and there seemed to be an artificial feeling about the place. "This doesn't seem like a place you would live," she said as she looked at the paintings and decorations. "Like I'm trying to force it?" he said, jokingly. She didn't respond, because that was exactly how it felt.

Summer followed as he led her upstairs, stopping in front of one of the bedrooms. It was organized with a full sized bed, nightstand, tall dresser and generic paintings on the wall. "This looks like a guest room," she said, as she looked around. "I guess you could say that," he responded before leaving her bag on the bed. As Summer unpacked her bag, she noticed the clothes in the dresser. There were already socks and underwear, pants, and shorts folded in the dresser. The closet had several t-shirts, skirts, and sleepwear. Clearly this room was setup to board a woman, but the selection of clothes were too generic to be personal. Honestly, she could give him credit, with what he provided, she wouldn't need to pack a single thing. Even the hygiene items were impressive, despite their lack of variety.

After she finished unpacking, she left the room, looking for David. To her surprise, the next room looked the same, although with different colored bedding and slightly different paintings. "Looking for me?" Summer gasped in surprise, "You scared the shit out of me!" "Sorry about that," he apologized. "So, you basically just run your home like a guest house?" "Not exactly," he answered. "I don't have children, and you never know who might show up." As Summer turned, she could see the inside of his room through the cracked door over his shoulder. "Is that your room?" she asked as she pushed past him. "Yes it is." He made no attempt to stop her, but her expectations seemed to be deflated.

"This room looks like the rest," she said as she scanned. The only difference was that this room was definitely occupied. There was a much bigger dresser, dirty clothes were in the hamper, the closet contained his clothing as well as others, clearly belonging to a woman. The bed was queen sized, and the paintings were more personal. "So, you and your wife share a bed?" she asked with a serious tone. He smiled as he left the room, "Why wouldn't we. Come downstairs when you've settled in, I'll make some dinner." Summer didn't bother changing, but made little adjustments to her room, putting her personal hygiene items in the bathroom before going downstairs.

David was in the kitchen, preparing food as she sat at the table. "So, why are you here?" he asked. "I'm taking a break for the summer, and I really wanted to see you." "Is that all?" he continued. "No, I had a really bad dream a few weeks ago and now I don't know what to do about it." David stopped, thinking for a moment before continuing, "What was your dream about?"

Summer talked through her dream, describing the smells, the emotion and the ungodly heat. David listened as he prepared to serve dinner, "That actually sounds very familiar, but when I went through it, I was in a much colder region, so I wasn't aware of the effects until a bit later." Summer looked at her food, "Are you going to try and stop it?" she asked. David shook his head, "I can't stop it, I can only prepare for it."

As Summer ate her food, she explained her feelings about college and her ideas for transferring her reserve unit, as David listened. "Where is your wife at?" Summer asked, as if it just dawned on her. Looking at his watch, he answered, "Should be here any minute now, she usually gets off work around 5:00pm." The two finished their food and Summer began washing the dishes when the door suddenly opened. "I'm home!" a woman's voice called out. Summer quickly turned, but before she could see who it was, the woman quickly ran up the stairs. Summer's heart sank as she finished the dishes. After drying her hands, she went into the living room and sat on the couch, as if waiting to be discovered.

As she waited, David descended the stairs and offered Summer a drink. "Can I have some coffee?" she asked. David was shocked, "When did you start drinking coffee?" "In college," she smiled. Summer could hear the shower upstairs as she waited for the coffee to get done, watching David from the couch. "Is it going to be okay if I stay here?" she asked. "Of course, why wouldn't it be," he yelled from the kitchen. David handed Summer her coffee and as they both sat in the living room, she could hear movement upstairs. Every second seemed to feel like an eternity as her heart began to sink with every footstep that vibrated through the floor above.

As the woman descended the stairs, Summer struggled to look up. Her head was a hurricane of emotions as dozens of scenarios and thoughts flooded her mind. "Summer!" the woman screamed. Still in shock, Summer was tackled by the woman as she sat on the couch. "Tiffany? Is that you?" Summer finally realized. "Yes! How are you, how was school?" Tiffany asked excitedly. Turning to David, Summer asked, "You married Tiffany?" David smiled, "This is her reward for her loyalty."

Chapter 16

The Younger Sister

The two girls spent the next few hours catching up. Apparently, Tiffany finished school the same year as their New Years Eve event, several months after David was assigned to his unit. That summer, he finally went back home to pick up his car and other possessions when he ran into Tiffany. Over dinner, she reminded David of his promise to reward her, and he agreed to marry her on three conditions. First, she must follow him, no matter where he went or what he did, no questions asked. Second, she must give him equal to one quarter of his pay to be used at his discretion. Third, she must accept her role as his property, and their marriage was only a legal contract, which could be amended or revoked at any time. However, he also promised to keep her regardless.

They had been married for nearly two years when Summer showed up, but Tiffany was told to expect something like this. She worked south of the base at a rancher's clinic, and at David's insistence, did not get involved in Family Readiness Group activities. "I already made dinner if you're hungry," David said. Tiffany jumped up and smiled before walking to the kitchen. Summer's heart began to settle as she sat back in her seat. "So, nothing's changed?" she asked. David shook his head, "No, nothing's changed."

Tiffany brought her food out to the living room and sat in the chair across from the couch. "Are you going to be sleeping with David while you're here?" Tiffany asked with a straight face. Summer nearly spit out her coffee at the question. "What the hell are you talking about?" she asked, still catching her breath. "Isn't he your husband? Why would I sleep with him?" Tiffany smiled while chewing on her food before sharing a look with David. "David doesn't belong to me, we belong to him." Tiffany's words struck Summer like a bolt of lightning. Just what kind of life was she stepping into. Better yet, what kind of life was she already a part of?

It was obvious that the roles were already established, and Tiffany was completely on board. Subconsciously, she had already accepted this, but she had never truly realized just how crazy it sounded until Tiffany said it so confidently. "It's okay, I just got here, so you can stay with him tonight," Summer said nervously. Tiffany smiled while still chewing her food, never breaking eye contact.

Later that night, as Summer took her shower, David could be heard through the wall, talking with Tiffany. As the water ran down her face, her imagination put her in Tiffany's position. What if it was her coming home to see Tiffany or even Jennifer sitting on the couch? Could she be so confident? Just then, the realization hit, she was going to be there with them until the end of the month. Summer turned off the water and wrapped a towel around her body, stepping out of the shower onto another towel, placed on the floor. She dried her hair using the blow dryer before walking into the room across the hall. Clothes were already laid out on the bed, something David must have done while she was in the bathroom.

As she got dressed, Tiffany stood in the doorway. "I hope you like the clothes I laid out for you." Summer smiled, "I thought maybe David laid them out." "Can I sit down?" Tiffany asked. "Sure, but you don't have to ask me as long as the doors open." Tiffany smiled as she sat down, "Then the same goes for you too." The two sat quietly on the bed for a few minutes. "How long did it take for you to get used to living like this?" Summer asked. Tiffany thought for a moment before answering, "I don't know if I ever really did, but it does get easier. David keeps saying that this isn't our real home yet, so I guess that helps." "Is it weird with me being here?" "No, not really. I was actually hoping for some company, especially since I've started to get used to being here." "Why is that?" Tiffany thought about how best to explain their situation. "Well, David is very focused, and believe it or not, we aren't just playing house."

Summer never truly thought about their unique arrangement. David's focus would always be guided by his knowledge of the future, and before Summer's dream, it had all seemed like a game they played together. However, since that day, she understood his determination more, why he trained so hard, why he was so cold, and even his need for control. "Do you think he sees us as equals, or are we just toys for him?" Summer asked. Tiffany smiled, placing her hand on Summer's, "I think he needs us just as much as we need him. You see, David is like a locomotive. His life is guided by the tracks that have already been laid in front of him, and I'm sure he could make it to his destination on his own, but what would he do once he got there?" Summer shrugged her shoulders. "We may not be driving this train, but as long as we give him what he needs to get there, we can all make it together."

Later that night, Summer was lying in her bed. David certainly spared no expense getting good mattresses, even the bedding was really comfortable. The more she thought, the more she considered Tiffany's words from earlier. David knew exactly what he was going to do, and at least Tiffany didn't have to worry about where her life was going, after all, she was married to him.

She looked at the clock, only 9:31pm, yet everyone was already in bed. Maybe she should go check and see what David and Tiffany are doing? As she left her room, the flood light from outside shined through the bathroom window, lighting up the floor in front of her room. As she tip toed down the hallway, she noticed the bedroom door was cracked. Quietly she pushed the door open, shutting it tightly behind her. She tried not to make a noise as she quietly slid into the bed on David's side, but as soon as she pulled his blanket over her, she felt his arms pull her close. "Goodnight Summer," he whispered as he kissed her on the forehead.

The next morning, she was woken up by David as he got ready to go to morning formation. "What time do you work today?" Summer asked. "10:30 until late, so you'll have the house to yourself for a while. She looked at the clock, it was 6:00am. Summer was surprised to see Tiffany wearing clothes next to her, still asleep. Suddenly, she was struck by a surge of motivation. She quickly jumped out of bed and ran downstairs, starting the coffee pot. As she sat waiting at the table, David came downstairs, first looking at the coffee pot, then at Summer. The smile he gave her nearly broke her on the spot. He was genuinely pleased with her, something she wasn't as prepared for as she thought.

As the coffee pot was still heating up, he approached her, holding out his hand. Placing her hand in his, she genuinely thought he was either going to kiss her hand or shake it. However, expectations versus reality are seldom the same. As soon as he took her hand, he stepped back, forcing her to stand on her feet. With the opposite hand, he reached in, grabbing her neck firmly as he kissed her hard on the lips. Her mouth naturally fell open, taking him in. He placed her hand behind his back as he reached forward, pulling her tight as he stepped into the doorway between the kitchen and the hallway.

With her back firmly against the door jamb, he pushed his hands up under her shirt and under her ass, causing her back to arch, favoring his intent. Summer wrapped her arms around his neck as she glided her tongue firmly along his. David lifted her up, pressing her body against the doorway as she wrapped her legs around his waist, waiting for his next move. Guided by his hand, he slid his cock inside of her, allowing her body weight to pull her down, thrusting him deep until she could feel him pressing against her cervix. Unapologetically, he fucked her hard against the narrow door jamb, as she held onto him, submitting to his actions.

Summer dripped onto the floor as David thrust his hips into her, pulling her panties with his right hand as he held her ass with the left. She felt like her head was finally out of the water as her senses kicked into overdrive. Struggling to hold it in as he rammed her repeatedly, her body involuntarily gave in as she began pouring herself onto the tile floor like a sopping wet dishtowel. As he finished, she tightened her grip, clenching down on him as he filled her up.

David sat her down and quickly washed off in the bathroom around the corner, just as Tiffany came down the stairs. Summer was still standing in the doorway, feet apart, hands resting on her knees with her head down as she tried to catch her breath. Just as David came walking back, Tiffany passed in front of Summer, slipping on the tile in front of her. Summer jumped and David caught Tiffany before she fell. "What the hell did I just slip on?" Tiffany asked confused. David chuckled as Summer blushed. Studying the other two, Tiffany smiled as she looked down at the floor. "Don't look at it, I'll clean it up!" Summer said defensively.

As David poured his coffee, Summer was wiping the floor and Tiffany was getting out the toaster. "Does anyone else want some breakfast?" Tiffany asked. Summer raised her hand, still refusing to look up as David leaned over to kiss Tiffany. "Not right now, I've got to go," he said as he prepared to leave. David kissed Summer on the way out the door, leaving Summer and Tiffany in the kitchen. "Breakfast?" Tiffany smiled. "Thank you, that'd be great," Summer responded, still embarrassed.

Later that afternoon, Summer was sitting on the couch, waiting for the other two to come when the door finally opened. "I'm home!" Tiffany yelled as she ran up the stairs to take a shower. Summer stood up and went to the kitchen to start making dinner, even though she wasn't a particularly good cook, David certainly made it easy with his meal prep and menu based shopping. As she was preparing to plate the food, Tiffany came back downstairs. "Good afternoon, did you have fun today?" she asked. "I guess, but I didn't think there was much to do. I managed to get all the laundry done, but everything else is pretty much finished." Tiffany smiled, "It's even harder when he isn't home, sometimes it feels like we're just waiting on him."

Summer thought for a moment. "Well, at least I have my drill time next weekend, that's something to look forward to," she said as she played with her food. Tiffany cupped her hand. "It only feels like this now, because you're visiting, once you move in permanently, I'm sure we'll have much more fun together." Summer smiled as she began eating her food. "What time does he usually get home at night?" "Usually at 8:00pm, every other day, otherwise, he's home before I am." Summer and Tiffany finished their dinner. As Tiffany cleaned the dishes, Summer asked, "Should we save some dinner for him?" "No, he'll eat at work, let's just make sure everything is clean by the time he gets home.

After dinner, Summer went upstairs to take a bath. While sitting in the bathtub, she heard a knock at the door. "Hey Summer," Tiffany said as she poked her head in the door. "Hey Tiffany, you can come in if you want." Tiffany walked into the bathroom and immediately removed her clothes. "I meant in the bathroom, not the bathtub!" Summer exclaimed. "Relax, we need to talk anyway."

As the two sat in the bathtub facing each other, Summer was the first to speak. "Do you think David will ever want to live a normal life?" "What are you talking about, what is normal anyway?" Summer sighed, "You know, like having children and stuff." "Do you want to have children?" Tiffany asked. "Eventually, but you're older, so I figured you would have thought about it too." Tiffany smiled, "I have thought about it." "And?" "And, David was very specific about his twenty-five percent rule. So, how am I supposed to provide that if I don't work?" Summer thought for a moment, "So you just pay him? Is that how you contribute?" Tiffany shook her head, "No we both share the living expenses, this is for something else." "Are you allowed to ask what it's for?" "No," Tiffany shook her head. "Once I give it to him, it's not mine anymore." "Well, what does he do with all of his money?" Summer asked curiously. "Well, we don't exactly buy a lot of fancy stuff, and he's pretty picky about stuff we do buy. Plus, he saves a lot of his own money. I think that's what it's for."

Summer understood why David wouldn't give, after all, if she could prevent her dream from becoming a reality, who knows how far she would go. "So, when would you ever get a chance to have children?" Summer asked. Tiffany smiled, as if she had been waiting for a chance to answer. "When someone else was able to cover my share." Summer was stunned, she had no idea it could be that simple. "So, if I moved in and started working, you could quit your job and start having babies?" Tiffany laughed, "Not quite, but you aren't that far off. Children can be expensive and in order to secure our future with him, it only cost us a little each month." Summer leaned forward, "What if I wanted to have children?" "You could have children now if you wanted." "No, I still have a military obligation and besides, he's supposed to be moving before my contract ends."

Summer drained the bathtub and grabbed a towel, while Tiffany dried off her body and put her clothes back on. Before Tiffany left the bathroom, she turned back to Summer, "We're practically sisters, so we need to take care of each other from here on out." Tiffany's words warmed Summer's heart. She had never had a sibling and to be called a sister made her feel at home. That night, David got home and immediately took a shower. He had to work early in the morning, so getting to bed early was a priority. That night and for the rest of the week, Summer slept with David and Tiffany slept in Summer's room, however, every morning when they woke up, all three were in bed together.

The weekend of drill, Tiffany let Summer drive her car, as she had no idea how to drive a stick. During that weekend, David played the role of a house husband, making breakfast for Summer before she left each morning. By the end, the weekend was ending and she even managed to make several contacts at the hospital. Summer and Tiffany had grown closer during her time there, even sharing moments with David in the same bed. The last weekend before Summer's return, the three had a talk.

"Have you decided what you're going to do?" he asked. "Yes, I'm going to finish my degree and serve out my reserve time at home," Summer said. "That's good," nodding his head. "Why is that good?" she asked. "I need you to trust me on this," he responded coldly. "Your unit won't deploy until after your contract ends, so you'll be able to finish your degree without interruption, plus, I'm taking leave next month, Tiffany is going to need some help while I'm in class." "What kind of class are you taking?" Summer asked. "Some kind of Sergeant's school," Tiffany responded. "It's the Primary Leadership Development Course, and it's thirty days. I won't be able to leave, and I want everyone to stay as close to home as possible." Summer and Tiffany were confused. "Why is that so important," Summer asked. "It's not really that important, but my first day is on the eleventh of September, and I promise, you will never forget that day." Summer and Tiffany were concerned at David's sudden shift in tone.

"Will you tell us why that day is so important?" Tiffany asked. "I can't, but I don't want you to think less of me for keeping this to myself," he said seriously. Tiffany leaned close to him. "If you're right and it's as memorable as you say, then I promise not to be mad, but if you're wrong, it might change what I think about you." David smiled, "In this case, I really do hope I'm wrong."

As Summer prepared to leave, she reflected on her time with David and Tiffany. His demanded contribution wasn't a lot, but if she could endure for a few more years, she could help provide a sense of comfort for their bizarre family. Meanwhile, David would continue to guide each of them in the future. After arriving at her father's house, she was suddenly motivated to paint, remembering the hotel style paintings in David's house. If she was going to contribute, the least she could do was to make her future home more inviting.

One afternoon in early July, she decided to visit an old friend, driving to the plant nursery and seed shop downtown. As she parked her car, she stared out the window, imagining her future on a farm, sharing a single man while women ran around tending to different tasks. Shaking her head, she got out and walked into the store. "Good afternoon, I'm looking for someone that might work here." The man at the counter was almost shocked to see the woman in front of her. He was used to seeing dusty farmers and housewives clad in gardening attire, certainly not someone as cleanly dressed as her. "Who are you looking for?" he asked. "A short blonde named Jennifer?" Summer answered. "Are you two sisters?" he asked. Summer smiled, remembering her conversation with Tiffany. "I guess you could say that," she said with a smile.

The man went to the back as Summer walked around the store, admiring the plants and seed bins. "Krystal!" a voice called out. Summer recognized the voice, turning toward it. Jennifer was standing near the back door, wearing brown coveralls and a scarf on her head. "Jennifer!" she called out. "Summer, It's you!" Jennifer exclaimed excitedly. "I thought he said my sister was here," she said as she hugged Summer. Summer smiled. "I'll explain that later, can we talk?" Summer asked. After looking around, Jennifer nodded, "Come to the back with me, I still have work to do."

Summer followed Jennifer to the back of the store, revealing a long greenhouse lined with trees and plants. "So, what do you do here?" Summer asked. "I take care of the plants, but this is just a job for now. I'm still working on my Associate of Applied Sciences in Horticulture." Summer raised her eyebrows. "It seems like David is building a team after all," Summer said with a smile. "What?" Jennifer was confused. "Never mind, when was the last time you spoke with David?" she asked. Jennifer thought for a moment, "Maybe after the holidays, he was also here two summers ago, but after that, I only saw him that one time."

Summer sat on a stool, taking a deep breath before deciding on where to take the conversation. "I just got back from visiting him a few days ago and I think he's coming here next month." Jennifer nodded her head, "I think he did mention that once, something important, but he wouldn't tell me why." Summer smiled, she wanted to give details but remembered the last time she told Jennifer something, after David told her not to. "Did you know he got married?" Jennifer stopped, completely taken aback. "He's married?" Jennifer asked, as if in denial. "Yes, I spent the month with both of them at his home," Summer continued. "Who is she?" Jennifer asked, a hint of jealousy in her voice. Summer took a deep breath before continuing. "It's Tiffany, he married Tiffany."

Jennifer smiled, letting out a deep breath. "Oh, that's all?" Summer was shocked at her response. "You aren't upset?" she asked. "Why would I be upset? I can't assume he abandoned me, just because he married someone, that's a bad habit to get into." Summer didn't understand the source of her confidence. "I was heartbroken when I first found out, how can you be so calm?" Summer asked. Jennifer put her tools down, looking Summer in the eye. "Did you guys' fuck?" Summer blushed slightly as she answered, "Yes, a lot." "What about Tiffany?" "No, why would I fuck Tiffany?" Summer stammered. "Hahaha, no, how did she take it?" Summer immediately thought about the incident in the dining room, her ears turning red at the thought. "We've actually become quite close, she even called me her sister." Jennifer smiled, "That's a good way to look at it."

Chapter 17

Sleeping Arrangements

Several weeks later, David and Tiffany arrived, deciding to travel by car, so they were both exhausted from the trip. Their first stop was Connie's house. She knew about her daughter's marriage and despite her protest at the lack of ceremony, welcomed David as if their union was inevitable. He only spent one night there before leaving Tiffany to go to his hometown, several hours away. His mother had gotten a new job and was hardly home, as his father had been left at home to take care of David's younger brother. To David's surprise, his change in behavior did actually have an impact in his father's life for the better, but not in a way that would give David a great deal of hope.

David unpacked his bag in his old room which had been turned into a short term storage location. In his past life, his father had compulsively decided to renovate their home, leaving the family in chaos as unfinished projects and sloppy construction techniques left the house in a perpetual state of rapid decay. This time, with David's help, minor renovations were compartmentalized, and wild ideas were discarded. David's father had become more involved with the church, and he even started a landscaping business on the weekends. His younger brother was on summer break and would start his first year of high school in the fall, working through his summer for his father's landscaping company.

As David unpacked, his brother was in the garage, cleaning the yard equipment while his father slept, as he was still working at the packing plant during the week. His mother was on the road and wouldn't return for several days, so David left after unpacking, not wanting to waste time on formalities. He first went to Summer's father's house, curious about her adjustment back to her old ways.

After knocking on the door, Summer's reception was more relaxed than he remembered. Rather than jumping at him or lowering her head, she embraced him, kissing him long and deeply as if he had come home from a business trip. She guided him to her room where she had been working for the past few weeks, painting portraits, buildings and landscapes. David was a pop art painter that preferred acrylic paint, while Summer was an abstract realism painter that preferred watercolor, however, he had never painted this time around and only he knew. As he admired her work, Summer talked about her classes and even mentioned her own plans for their future.

As a pharmacist, she would have access to drugs and medications that could be useful, however, may not be available to the public without a prescription. Additionally, her growing knowledge of remedies may be beneficial in situations when medicines weren't available. Additionally, Summer had given Jennifer a list of plants to look out for. "I'm really impressed, it seems like you've really found an important role," David said, smiling. Summer glanced over at David, a look of fear in her eye, "Don't get carried away now, I don't want my dad walking in on you fucking me in my room." David chuckled, "Don't worry, I wouldn't put you in that position."

"Are you here to pick up Jennifer?" she asked. "Yes, but I have a week, then we'll pick up Tiffany on the way out." "Wait, Tiffany isn't with you?" she asked. "No, I dropped her off at her mother's house on the way here." Summer smiled. "When do you go back to class?" he asked. "September 4th," she responded. "When do you have Drill time?" "I had it last weekend, but my month of active duty is next week," she said after letting out a deep breath.

David sat on her bed, watching Summer paint for several minutes. Suddenly, as if prompted by nothing at all, she set her pallet and brushes down, sitting next to David on the bed. "Can I ask you a few questions?" David grabbed her hand, "Yes, you can ask, but I can't promise to answer all of your questions." "How did you become a Sergeant so fast?" David chuckled, "I thought you were going to ask me a difficult question." "It's just a warmup," she said. "Okay, let's see. I max my PT tests, I've memorized pretty much every policy and regulation, plus, I was a really good soldier last time too, so this time, it's a cake walk." Summer nodded her head. "Tiffany said it was difficult sometimes, what did she mean?" "Well, I spend more time than most doing weapon's training, and I like to go out with the LRSD team occasionally, so I'm out a lot." Summer wondered. "What's a LRSD team?" she asked. "It's the Long Range Surveillance Detachment, kind of like a ranger group within the Intelligence world."

"How long are you going to have to work before you start putting your plan into action?" she asked. "Wow, that's actually a good question. Let's see. Technically, I've already started, but if you're asking about groundbreaking work, then nine years. I hope to be completely finished in at least fifteen." Summer smiled, "Another question, Tiffany said you were saving money, so, how much have you saved so far?" David thought, "You understand that I need a lot of capital to do this right?" he asked. "I do, and I'm not trying to overstep, but I want to feel more included," she asked hesitantly. "It's fine, I don't mind. So far, I think I have almost $44 thousand saved." Summer took a deep breath. "Final question, do you love me?" David smiled, "I'll let you figure that one out on your own for now," he said quietly.

Summer kissed David on the corner of his mouth before leaning her head on his shoulder. "I want to marry you too," she said quietly. David turned to kiss her before responding. "You will." After sharing another long kiss, David stood as if preparing to leave. "I need to go talk to Jennifer's mother now." Summer looked up at him, "Okay, let me know how it goes." As David left, Summer picked up her brushes again, staring intently at her current work.

David arrived at Jennifer's house late in the afternoon after she had just got home. After knocking on the door, Jennifer came running as soon as she saw him through the window. "David!" she screamed as she opened the door. Jumping into his arms, he carried her into the house as she hung by his shoulders. "Good afternoon Laura," he called out. "Good afternoon David," she yelled from the kitchen. "Can I take everyone to dinner tonight?" he asked. Jennifer climbed down and began jumping excitedly as Laura watched the show. "Sure, but we'll need time to get ready," Laura answered. As Laura went to change, Jennifer immediately jumped in David's lap. "Master, I've missed you so much," Jennifer said as she nuzzled her head into his neck. As David pet her with his free hand, he whispered, "Go and get ready, we have something important to discuss."

Nearly an hour later, as the three sat down to eat, David ordered appetizers along with drinks for him and Jennifer. Laura sat across the table from the two of them, occasionally looking up from her menu, as her daughter shamelessly canoodled David in front of her. "I don't know why you two aren't a couple yet. I mean, she obviously likes you and you're always looking after her," Laura said with a resigned expression. David, unresponsive to Jennifer's affections, responded, "That's actually why I invited you two out, I wanted to talk about that." After their appetizers arrived, everyone placed their orders and Laura stared intently at David from across the table.

"I'm going back at the end of the week and I'm taking Jennifer with me," he said with a straight face. Laura was almost shocked while Jennifer looked as if she might spontaneously combust on the spot. "Just like that?" she asked. David nodded, "Yes, just like that. She can transfer her education and since I already have a house, she'll move in immediately." Jennifer's body seemed to shrink as a smile nearly cleaved her head in two. "Are you going to get married, or are you just planning on living together?" Laura asked seriously. "I understand your concerns, and I will marry her, but I have no intention of making it public." He responded coldly. Laura sighed. "If you do, I want pictures and an invitation. David nodded his head. With Laura's acceptance, Jennifer climbed on David, nearly spilling his drink as she fought to kiss him in the booth. David handed Jennifer a piece of paper with instructions written on it after he dropped

her and her mother off at home, before going back to his parents'
house.

Early the next morning, Jennifer went to work and handed
in her notice. It was a prewritten note with an empty signature
block provided by David. After reading it, her boss simply shook
her hand and wished her luck. On the way home, she drove to
the local college and withdrew, providing the registrar with a
forwarding address for her transcripts. After leaving the college,
she stopped by the bank and closed her accounts, receiving a
cashier's check for the balance from both her checking account
and savings account. Before going back home, she picked up an
address forwarding form from the post office. As she got home,
she excitedly went inside and started making lunch. The last thing
on her list was to pack, making sure she grabbed her social
security card, birth certificate and her final pay stub from work.

Meanwhile, David had woken up early to exercise,
stopping to invite Summer out while he was on his run, to which
she reluctantly agreed. Every time he would get a block ahead of
her, he would start doing lunges until she caught up. No wonder
she couldn't keep up with him in bed. Summer whined on the
way back, so he carried her piggyback the whole way as he ran
two miles back to her house. In Summer's kitchen, they both got
a drink of water. "What time did you start your workout this
morning?" she asked. David looked at his watch. "Probably
around 5:30am," he responded. Summer looked at the clock on
the oven. "It's nearly 7:40am, does that mean you've been
exercising more than an hour before you showed up?" she asked,
still catching her breath. David nodded. "I'm going to take a

shower," she said, finishing her water. David didn't respond as she walked toward the bathroom.

As David finished his water, he prepared to leave. "David!" Summer shouted from the bathroom. "What is it?" he asked. "Come help me please!" she answered. David followed the sound of her voice until he saw summer peeling off her shorts in the bathroom with the door open. Shrugging his shoulders, he walked in behind her. After he shut the door, Summer turned on the shower, then turned to face David. As he admired her pale skin, damp with sweat, she reached out and began lifting off his shirt, pressing her body against his as she struggled to pull his shirt off of his head. Not willing to pass up such an opportunity, he licked her neck as she stood close. Stepping back, she shot him a shameful glance before kneeling to remove his shoes and shorts.

As they both stood naked, she grabbed his dick and led him to the shower, like it was a leash. Once inside, he washed her body, as she held onto him, watching the water trickle off his skin. As she turned around, she reached back, holding his hips as he washed her back, kissing her on the neck. David's washing process was just as Summer expected, systematic and methodical, but she enjoyed it, nonetheless. As David stood, waiting for his turn, Summer massaged his body using her loofa as she kissed him everywhere she could reach. When she lowered herself to her knees, she guided her mouth over his cock while holding onto his thighs, never once using her hand for support. Summer's technique wasn't aggressive or too gentle, keeping a steady rhythm as she used her mouth to jerk him off.

Before he could reach for the back of her head, she stood up, kissing him passionately before resting her back against the wall. David continued to kiss her as she put her feet up on the alcove, straddling her legs around his. David knelt down and buried his tongue inside of her, sucking her labia and kissing her clit. As she thrust her hips forward, he began rhythmically swishing her pussy around in his mouth, sucking and licking simultaneously as she gripped his head firmly. David felt her cum several times before she started pushing his head away. As he stood, her eyebrows furrowed as she bit her lip, itching for him to fuck her. With her legs supported on the alcove, he effortlessly slid his dick inside of her, resulting in an immediate orgasm. David smiled as he grabbed her firmly, fucking her like a cheap whore.

Summer didn't try to hold anything back, as he repeatedly thrust his cock into her. She released one orgasm after another, until they eventually just blurred together. Even after he came inside of her, he never slowed down, fucking her as her very soul drained from her body. Eventually, Summer's body went limp. David held her as he laid her down in the shower, so he could finish rinsing off before turning off the water. He grabbed a towel and dried off, then wrapped her in a towel, carrying her limp body to her room. After drying her off, he left her on the bed and put his clothes in the washer. It was still early, so there was a good chance her father wouldn't be home anytime soon.

After returning, he laid next to her, holding her until she eventually woke up, nearly fifteen minutes later. Summer smiled as she looked into his eyes, rubbing his cheek with her hand. "How did I get in bed?" she asked. "You kind of passed out in the shower," he said. Summer didn't blush, but she was acting spaced out. "Are you okay?" he asked. "I've never been better," she answered, nodding her head. David kissed her and she buried her head under his chin. "I love you," she whispered. "I know," he responded, kissing her on the head.

David eventually moved his clothes to the dryer, while Summer stayed in her bed. Upon his return, he found her propped up on one elbow, covered up and staring at him as he entered the room completely naked. "What are you smiling about?" he asked. "Come here and lay down with me," she said coquettishly. David was happy to oblige. "Can I tell you a secret?" she asked. "You can, but is it a secret I'm supposed to keep, or is it a confession?" Summer rolled her eyes before continuing. "I actually kind of liked you when we were kids." "Really?" he asked in a surprised voice. "Yeah, but I was young and didn't know how to deal with it, so when you stopped talking to me, I just assumed you were going to just hate me forever." David smiled. "Can I confess something to you?" Summer smiled. "Please do." "I actually did, I didn't know why you turned against me so unexpectedly, so I just shut you out." "What changed?" she asked. "Well, my memory likes to replay all of my experiences, and I realized I reacted immaturely, plus I've been through a lot of therapy. So, when you confessed to me that day, I realized I had to forgive you."

The two continued to lay in bed and neither moved until the dryer buzzer went off. As David got up to get his clothes from her dryer, she also got out of bed and got dressed. When David returned, Summer was sitting on the edge of her bed smiling. "What are you smiling about now?" he asked. "When we were in bed together, I actually wanted to have sex again, but I couldn't move my legs, and when I got up to get dressed, I nearly fell." David raised his eyebrows. "Do you need me to stay?" he asked. "No, you've got things you need to do, besides, if you do stay, how am I going to explain to my father why I need a wheelchair?" David chuckled before kissing her goodbye.

After several days, David's leave was coming to an end, and it was almost time to go back. Jennifer waited for David, but she had not seen him since the day he took her and her mother to dinner, so when he showed up at her house that morning, she was more than ready to go. As Jennifer left her house, he was surprised at the lack of bags she had packed. "Is this all you have?" he asked. "No, I have another box in my room, but I couldn't carry it out," she answered. David went in to get the box, and upon entering her room, noticed that there were still clothes in the closet, bedding on the bed, and other things in her room. Obviously she didn't pack like she was moving, but rather, like she was visiting.

After putting the rest of her stuff in the trunk, Jennifer buckled into the passenger seat and excitedly waited for them to leave. David looked at her, "You didn't pack everything and you're acting like we're going on a trip. What is it you think is happening here?" he asked. Jennifer smiled. "My dreams are finally coming true," she said excitedly. "I don't need to take everything because that was my old life, and this is my new life, so I don't want to look back." David smiled, satisfied with her response. As they drove to Connie's house, David and Jennifer sang loudly as music played on the radio. If Summer reflected

David's intentions, then Jennifer reflected his playfulness, something he enjoyed about her.

"Master? Can I ask you a question?" "Of course you can," David responded. "Can I name our first baby after you?" she asked without hesitation. David thought for a moment. "I don't mind, but is that something you really want to do, or are you just feeling compelled?" "I don't know, I just thought of it," she answered. "By the way, are you just going to keep calling me Master, like it's my given name?" he asked. Jennifer smiled. "As long as you let me," she said with a smile. David never told Jennifer that he married Tiffany, yet he seemed unbothered at the potential calamity if this information were discovered, after all, he didn't feel that it was his responsibility to coddle them.

Early in the afternoon, David arrived at Connie's house. As the two of them walked toward the door, Tiffany came running out, jumping into David's arms as she reached him. "How was your visit?" he asked. "It was good, but I really, really missed you," she responded. As she let him go, she leaned down and hugged Jennifer, kissing her on the cheek. Jennifer blushed as they walked toward the house. "She's like a mother hen," Jennifer said as she touched her cheek. David smiled. "You two are going to get along really well," he said as they reached the door.

As Tiffany entered the house with David and Jennifer behind her, Connie ran to greet David, hugging him as he removed his shoes. "Welcome back David, I so wish you could have stayed longer last time," she said. David hugged Connie back, even though he didn't like hugging people, which anybody who knew David knew. Connie made coffee for her guests and upon sitting down, addressed the elephant in the room. "Who is this little girl, is she your sister?" Tiffany chuckled at her mother's question. "Yes mom, she's family, but she had to finish school," winking at Jennifer. Jennifer smiled and thanked Connie for the coffee. The three enjoyed dinner together, while engaging in idle chit chat.

As it got late, Connie announced the sleeping arrangements. "Tiffany, you and your husband can sleep in your room together. Jennifer dear, I don't have another bed, so you can either sleep with me, or on the couch." Jennifer lowered her head. "Miss Connie, is it okay if I sleep in the same room as them?" Connie, not wanting to be rude, answered with an exaggerated sense of sincerity. "I think it's best if the married couple have a room for themselves." "I don't mind!" Tiffany interjected. "Are you sure dear?" Connie asked in a concerned tone. "Absolutely, plus, she's in a new place and we don't want her losing sleep over it." Connie acquiesced and after everyone took a shower, got ready for bed.

The next morning, David and Tiffany woke up early. As Tiffany made breakfast, David attempted to wake up Jennifer. "Did you see Summer when you were there?" Tiffany asked. "Yes I did, she's actually started painting portraits for the house," he answered. "Did you two have fun without me?" she asked teasingly. He set his coffee down and leaned close, whispering in Tiffany's ear. "I made her cum so hard, she fainted." Tiffany smiled. "I want to do that when we get home!" she said excitedly. David simply smiled, taking another drink of his coffee. As the three left the house, David drove, as Jennifer slept in the back seat. "Maybe she had trouble sleeping," Tiffany said, looking back at her.

Chapter 18

Ritualistic Behavior

As the three headed back, Tiffany had begun to relish in her role as a passenger princess, a benefit she only earned due to her inability to drive David's car. Meanwhile, Jennifer traded out with David every time they stopped, whether it was for a meal, for a bathroom break, or simply to stretch. If they drove straight through, they could have made it in less than twenty hours, however, both girls begged David to stay overnight once they got halfway there. As the sun went down, Tiffany and Jennifer stared out the window, hoping to find a hotel for them to stay. Not wanting to waste time, David exited within the first big city they passed along their route, stopping at a large hotel, just off the highway.

As the girls brought in their bags, David got a room, receiving more looks of envy from the hotel staff and guests, as the two women clung to his arms. Once they reached their floor, David handed Jennifer the key and watched as she skipped down the hall to their room, holding open the door. Once inside, all three began taking out their hygiene items, placing them in the bathroom before settling in. David told Jennifer to shower first, as he ordered food from the menu on the nightstand. Tiffany looked at Jennifer suspiciously as she shamelessly removed her clothes, flaunting her body in front of David as if she were trying to provoke him.

Not to be outdone, Tiffany unceremoniously removed her clothes from bottom to top, as he hung up the phone. "There's no reason for you to be jealous," he said. Tiffany smiled as she crawled onto him. "Why would I be jealous? Besides, I haven't been fucked by you for nearly a week, and I need you to remind me who I am," she said playfully. As Jennifer finished her shower, she wrapped herself in a towel and quickly dried her hair. Before leaving the bathroom, she put on her chemise and choker, hoping to seduce David while Tiffany took a shower.

As Jennifer left the shower, she gasped at the sight of Tiffany being brutally fucked on the edge of the bed, as if David was trying to split her in half. "Oh shit!" Jennifer said, hocked at his unbridled aggression. Tiffany looked at Jennifer through teary eyes as David held her neck and the back of her hair firmly against the bed, while her leg lifelessly hung over his shoulder. Her body seemed to have gone through hell; her hair was disheveled, her skin was riddled with handprints and her eyes had the look of a woman that had simply given up. As David noticed Jennifer, he smiled, immediately dismounting her, then walked around to Tiffany's head. "Turn over," he commanded. Tiffany looked almost afraid to refuse as she clumsily rolled onto her back, looking up at him. "Open your mouth and clean up your mess," he ordered. Tiffany fearfully licked and sucked his cock, trying to remove any trace of anything she may have left on him as he intentionally made it difficult for her.

Once she was done, he reached down, grabbing her jaw as he leaned close to her face. "Go take a fucking shower, you filthy slut," he growled in a low voice. Jennifer nearly came on the spot watching this. Without looking at anyone, Tiffany rushed to the bathroom, grabbing a handful of clothes on the way. "What the fuck was that?" Jennifer asked. "What the fuck was what?" David retorted, smiling. Jennifer's seductive initiative was immediately quenched at the sight she just saw, unsure if Tiffany did or said something to anger him. Without saying a word, she sat next to him, leaning against his shoulder as he held her close.

Suddenly the phone rang. "Hello. yes, of course. I'll be down in five minutes." David hung up the phone. "Who was that?" Jennifer asked. "Our food is here, I'll be right back." He quickly got dressed and left the room. Jennifer didn't move as she sat quietly, listening to the shower running in the bathroom. After only a few minutes, he returned carrying two bags in his hand, along with a drink tray. As he set the drinks down, Tiffany came out of the shower, drying her hair. "Did you get my mushroom burger?" she asked. David handed over her food, followed up by an intimate kiss from Tiffany. "What the fuck is going on?" Jennifer asked, confused by the sight. Tiffany smiled at Jennifer as she took a bite of her hamburger.

"Did she get in trouble or something?" Jennifer asked. "God I hope so," Tiffany responded, still chewing on her food. Jennifer sighed in exasperation. "You two scared the shit out of me." David smiled at Tiffany, who then leaned to kiss David again, "Thank you sir," she whispered. The three ate their food as Tiffany continued smiling at David. Meanwhile, Jennifer watched both of them curiously, wondering what kind of bizarre kinks those two were into. After they finished eating, David went to take a shower, leaving the girls alone in the room.

"Tiffany, can I ask you a question?" "Sure," Tiffany responded. "Is there an order to how this is supposed to go?"

Tiffany thought for a moment. "You and Summer seem to have the same concerns, but no, there isn't. I may have married David first, but as I told her, he doesn't belong to me, we belong to him." "Oh, sorry if my questions are annoying," Jennifer said as she lowered her head. Tiffany raised her chin. "Don't apologize, we're in this together, and our focus needs to be on him." Jennifer smiled. "Thank you Madam Tiffany." Tiffany blushed at the title. "You don't have to call me Madam." "Oh, yes I do," Jennifer insisted. "I like the structure we have, and I don't want to be anything more than his pet." Tiffany smiled, petting Jennifer on the head. "Then I guess it's okay with me."

David finally got out of the shower, and after seeing Tiffany petting Jennifer, he asked, "Are you two getting along?" "Yes Master!" Jennifer smiled. Tiffany chuckled as David sat down. "It seems like I've been dubbed the matriarch by the other two," Tiffany said jokingly. David turned to her. "If that's the responsibility you want, then you need to own it," he said with a serious tone. Suddenly his words sounded in her heart like a gong, he didn't dismiss it as she thought he would. Suddenly, Tiffany's world seemed to grow in an instant, and the thought of carrying such a title filled her with a sense of pride.

The three fell asleep in the same bed, tired from their long trip. As the morning sun began to shine through the window, David woke up to Jennifer riding him. Her eyes were closed, and she didn't seem to notice that he was awake. "Having fun up there?" he asked. Jennifer immediately looked down at him, smiling as she leaned over to kiss him, "Good morning Master, I hope you're not mad," she said quietly. "No, carry on," he responded, watching her as she gently moved her body on top of his. Trying not to be noticed, he reached his hand out and squeezed Tiffany's arm, waking her up. Tiffany saw Jennifer and covered her mouth, as if she wasn't supposed to see what Jennifer was doing. As Tiffany tried to suppress her laughter, Jennifer reached down and grabbed Tiffany's breast, rolling her nipple between her fingers.

Tiffany's shocked face nearly made David laugh, as he watched his pet fondling his matriarch. Tiffany mouthed the words, what should I do, as Jennifer seemed to become more aggressive. David shrugged his shoulders, eliciting a frown from Tiffany at his indifference. David reached down between Tiffany's legs and began massaging her clit as Tiffany tried to stifle her moans. David continued to tease her as Jennifer smiled down at them, never breaking her rhythm. Tiffany kissed David as he fingered her, all while Jennifer continued to fuck David. As Jennifer came, she slowly laid her body on the opposite side and put her arm over Tiffany, kissing David on the cheek. As Tiffany turned to look at Jennifer, Jennifer kissed Tiffany as well. "Good morning Madam Tiffany," she whispered. David, amused by the spectacle, hugged them both, kissing both of them before laying his head back.

The three eventually got out of bed, quickly showering and getting dressed. As David checked out of their room, Jennifer put their bags in the trunk of the car and Tiffany was getting breakfast downstairs. Eventually, David and Jennifer joined her, not saying a word. Back on the road, David drove first, as Tiffany laid down in the back seat and Jennifer marked their route in the road atlas.

The three finally arrived in the late evening, as David parked in front of his home. "This is your house?" Jennifer asked. "Don't get too excited, it's a quad, so we share the building with three other neighbors," he responded. Together, all three entered the house, one after the other. Tiffany ran upstairs, claiming the shower as David stopped to make coffee in the kitchen. The house seemed unusually quiet as Jennifer sat at the dining room table. "This house seems impersonal, kinda like you," she said, smiling at him. "Come upstairs, I'll show you the bedrooms," he said, gesturing her to go.

As she arrived on the second floor, she immediately looked into the first bedroom. "Which one did Summer stay in?" she asked, looking back at David. "She actually stayed in this one, when she wasn't in my room," he answered. Jennifer looked in the second bedroom. "This one looks the same." As she turned to face the last door, she looked back at David. "Is this your room?" He nodded. Jennifer pushed the door open, studying the furniture and the bed. "Does Tiffany sleep in here with you?" she asked. "Yes, she does, so you two need to come to an understanding on your own." Jennifer smiled before stopping at the bathroom door. "I like her," Jennifer said quietly.

David never bothered to explain any house rules, other than his standing order to not engage in gossip or to get involved with the Family Readiness Group, meanwhile, Tiffany showed Jennifer the rest of the house, and even helped her settle in. Jennifer took a bath and after putting on a pair of pajamas, examined the clothes stocked in the dressers and closet. The dresser had four drawers and stood four feet tall. Each drawer already containing standard clothing in light colored cotton fabric, however, there wasn't a single bra. The closet was nearly empty with only nineteen various shirts, sweaters and sleepwear, as well as a down jacket. Jennifer smiled as she added her own clothes to the collection.

After going downstairs, she saw Tiffany and David talking on the couch. "What are you guys talking about?" she asked. Tiffany, who had her feet tucked under her, took a sip of her coffee before responding. "We're making a grocery list, so if you want to give your input, now's the time." Jennifer sat right next to David, tucking her toes under his leg. "Can we get cereal? I noticed you don't have any." David thought for a moment, "What kind?" he asked. "Cheerios," she replied. David added it to the list as Tiffany smiled. "What is it?" Jennifer asked, feeling like she was missing something. "David doesn't usually get cereal, so this is a first."

They finished up the list and went to bed soon after. Jennifer stayed in her room that night, but found it very difficult to sleep, despite the bed being so comfortable. The next morning, as she walked down the stairs, David was cooking breakfast as Tiffany sat at the table, patiently waiting. "What's for breakfast?" she asked. "Bacon, eggs, potatoes and waffles," he answered. Jennifer sat excitedly at the table, now feeling kind of silly for suggesting cereal. The three ate breakfast together and brushed their teeth, preparing to go to the grocery store.

David directed Jennifer to get a second cart as Tiffany pushed the first. Tearing the list in half, he handed the bottom half to Tiffany. "Start on the opposite side and get everything you can. Jennifer, you come with me, we're starting on this side, then we'll meet in the middle." Tiffany took the list and immediately left for the other side of the store. "That's a big list, are we stocking up on food already?" she asked. "Kind of, I will be gone next month and while I'm gone, I don't want either of you going out," he answered. Jennifer nodded, feeling motivated by his orders. Within an hour, David met Tiffany in the pasta isle, finishing their shopping expedition. As they stood in line, David laid out his plans for the next month. They were going to food prep until the freezer was completely full, and at some point later that day, David was going to deposit Jennifer's cashier's checks into his account, while Tiffany continued to prepare food at home.

Once they reached the checkout, David and Tiffany began stacking the food on the conveyer belt in order from heaviest to lightest, grouping foods together by type and use. Jennifer watched, somewhat amused by this system he enforced. After they got home, they unloaded the groceries and David sent Jennifer to retrieve her checks as he gave instructions to Tiffany. His goal was to have at least 90 meals prepped by the end of the week, and with the meals already in the freezer, they weren't even halfway there.

David had Jennifer endorse both checks as he wrote his deposit information on the back. "We're not going to the bank?" she asked. "No, we don't have to, but you should keep track of your money, because no matter where it's held, it's still yours." Jennifer smiled as she kissed him. "I trust you, but I'll do as you say," she answered. After dropping off the checks in the outgoing mail, the three got to work in the kitchen. Tiffany continued to cut vegetables as David prepared the various meats. Jennifer was making waffles, stacking them in freezer bags as she finished them, one batch at a time. By dinner time, all of the vegetables were cut and stored, David had prepared three meats to marinade for the next 48 hours, and Jennifer made just over one hundred waffles, following David's recipe and instructions.

As they sat down to eat dinner, Jennifer smiled, feeling proud and enabled by her master. "So, are we just not going to cook for the next two months?" she asked. "No, we can still cook, but when time doesn't permit, or if we're on different schedules, this will alleviate that source of stress," he answered. Tiffany was already familiar with his food prep technique, as he spent months teaching her mother this same process when they were younger. "When I was in high school, he taught me and my mother about this. Apparently, this is something he learned when he was living alone," Tiffany said as she continued to eat her food.

Over the next several weeks, they eventually finished their food prep, and Tiffany took Jennifer shopping for personal items and clothes. The two grew closer as they spent time together, and David finally purchased a computer for the house. During the week, Jennifer stayed at home, tending to the garden she started shortly after arriving, while David and Tiffany went to work. The weekend of September eighth, David packed his uniforms and clothes for class, while the girls watched. Tiffany had requested a leave of absence for three weeks, starting on the 10th, citing her husband's absence as her rationale.

On the morning his class started, Tiffany dropped him off at his Battalion headquarters, kissing him as she told him goodbye. David hugged her as he whispered into her ear, "Don't be afraid, and take care of Jennifer when I'm gone. I'll be home next month." He kissed her deeply and got on the bus. His class was actually closer to his home than his Battalion headquarters, but because of the nature of the course, nobody was allowed to drive there on their own.

Later that morning, as David was still in-processing, his heart sank as he watched the television from across the room. "It does not appear that there is any kind of effort up there. Oh my God! That looks like a second plane. We just saw another plane come in from the side. You did, that was… Yes, so that was the second explosion, you could see the plane come in, just from the right hand side of the screen." David looked on, unsurprised as the news was broadcast. After sitting down, he immediately thought about everyone he cared about. He never bothered to ask what anyone thought, but he genuinely wondered what the girls were doing.

Meanwhile, neither Summer, nor Tiffany nor Jennifer were watching the news, but after word started to spread, they all eventually turned on the news. Jennifer cried as she watched the television, while Summer and Tiffany sat in shock. While they continued to watch as the story unfolded, one simple truth seemed to outshine everything they saw, everything David said was true. As Jennifer started to gain her composure, she noticed Tiffany's expression, which had become deathly serious after watching the news broadcast. "What are you thinking?" Jennifer asked. Tiffany sat back in her seat. "David. David knew this was going to happen," she answered solemnly. Jennifer stared as her expression became serious.

"What does that mean?" Jennifer asked. "It means that David was right about everything," she said, as she hugged

Jennifer. Meanwhile, Summer sat on the floor of her dorm room, thinking the same thoughts. She wanted to go to David immediately but remembered his words, she had to stay put for the time being. Things in the country began to change rapidly, airport security became more aggressive, and every military installation increased their force protection posture immediately. Fortunately, Tiffany and Jennifer were home and had no reason to leave for the next few weeks. As the month passed, Tiffany and Jennifer would visit the academy every weekend, only permitted to watch as his class held their formation in front of them. In response to David's prediction, Tiffany had started wearing her choker, something she hadn't done since prom night.

After class was over, Tiffany waited at the Battalion headquarters for David to be dismissed. He was required to attend a formation held by the Battalion Command Sergeant Major, where he issued his standard decree to his noncommissioned officers and promoted recent graduates. As the formation was released, David put his bag in the trunk of the car and waited in the passenger seat for Tiffany to take him home. "Are you okay?" he asked, concerned about her change in attitude over the past few weeks. Tiffany wiped tears from her eyes as she responded. "I want to give you a child," she said as she looked down. David smiled as he kissed her on the cheek. "Let's go home," he said.

Upon arriving home, David was met by Jennifer at the door, wearing a light blue babydoll dress and a choker. As he went upstairs to unpack his bag, Jennifer stopped him. Tiffany began unpacking his bag as Jennifer undressed him in his room. Neither said a word to him as they worked slowly and carefully, trying not to make any unnecessary noise. David found this behavior peculiar, even ritualistic as each one systematically tended to their individual tasks. Once he was completely undressed, Jennifer led him into the bathroom, where a bath was already running for him. There, Tiffany joined him in the tub, washing his skin gently, using a loofa and her own body, while Jennifer went to tend to other things.

David felt like a monarch in his own castle at the treatment he was receiving, but didn't dare question it. Whatever they were planning, he wanted to see it through. As he got out of the bath, Jennifer returned, patting him dry with a towel before walking him to her bed. There, she laid him down and began massaging his body when Tiffany entered the room, wearing a satin slip with a red choker. Together, both of them continued to massage him for the next half hour, filling his head with an array of inappropriate thoughts. Tiffany crossed the line first, sucking his cock as Jennifer continued to massage his chest and shoulders, eventually mounting him.

Tiffany and Jennifer took turns fucking him, each time cleaning him off as he shamelessly teased the other. As they finished treating him, David sat up, admiring each of them as they stood in front of him, waiting for his praise. After thanking and praising them both, he asked, "Am I supposed to walk around naked the rest of the day, or can I get some clothes?" "I'm okay with that," Jennifer responded confidently. Tiffany rolled her eyes and immediately brought David's clothes to him. Later that evening, all three ate dinner together and eventually went to bed.

Chapter 19

A Nurse's Disbelief

In the two years that followed, the three continued to live out their life, just as they had been, with some minor changes. Tiffany continued to work at the ranch until she ultimately quit her job after six months due to her pregnancy. Jennifer started college that first winter, hoping to finish her degree by the next year, while working at the Post exchange in the garden center. David was offered a conditional promotion to Staff Sergeant, but ultimately declined, as he felt it would throw his plans off track but was still sent to the Basic Noncommissioned Officer's Course that Summer. Due to an impending hurricane, he graduated without ceremony and immediately returned home.

Upon arriving at his house late that night, he quietly entered the living room, hoping to surprise everyone with his return. David tip toed upstairs and quietly entered the bathroom and brushed his teeth, but moments later, his surprise was cut short as Tiffany entered the bathroom, responding to nature's call. "David, you're home!" she said excitedly. "I thought you wouldn't be home for a few days." David spit into the sink before responding. "We can thank the hurricane for that one," he said as he smiled. "Is it going to be bad?" she asked. David shook his head. "No, it won't do anything here," he responded. Tiffany hugged his back as he finished brushing his teeth. "Did you know I was here, or did you come in here for something else?" he asked.

"Oh! I have to use the bathroom," she quickly responded before sitting on the toilet.

David sat on the alcove of the bathtub. "How has everyone been?" he asked, holding her hand. "We've been good, Jennifer got a promotion, and Aidan is getting into everything," she answered. "Are you sure you can handle him by yourself?" he asked in a concerned tone. "Yes, now please leave so I can finish." David kissed her before leaving, quietly entering his room. As he got undressed, his bed began to stir. "Go back to sleep, I'm not supposed to be home yet," he whispered. Jennifer turned on the bedside light and immediately jumped up. "The fuck I will!" she exclaimed, as she jumped into his arms.

Jennifer didn't even pretend to be modest with David, as soon as he set her down, she immediately removed her panties and shirt as if it were the most normal thing. David smiled before deciding to indulge her without hesitation. He never even bothered to shut the door as he lifted her legs by the calves, thrusting himself into her. As he finished, Tiffany stood in the doorway, watching the two. "Have you been there the entire time?" he asked. "The door was cracked," Tiffany responded. Jennifer jumped out of bed to use the bathroom, grabbing Tiffany to kiss her as she passed. "Ewe, you smell like sex you little whore!" Tiffany said as she pushed Jennifer away.

While Jennifer was in the bathroom, Tiffany sat next to David on the bed. "David, I've been thinking while you've been gone and now that I have Aidan, I've started to see things differently." David propped himself up on his elbows. "What are you trying to say?" he asked. Tiffany let out a deep sigh. "I want a divorce," she said seriously. David furled his eyebrow. "Just like that?" he asked. "Yes," she nodded. David thought for a moment before responding. "Okay, I'll make some phone calls tomorrow," he replied smiling. Jennifer returned from the bathroom and immediately grabbed Tiffany's tits from behind. "What are you two talking about?" she asked playfully. Pushing Jennifer's hands away, she responded coldly. "David and I are going to get a divorce."

Jennifer was shocked, looking at Tiffany and David, who seemed to be completely unbothered by the news. Thinking for a moment, she asked. "Don't you have to go back to the state you got married in to get a divorce?" David sighed, "No, technically you don't, but I'm going to call tomorrow and find out what our best options are." "What's the law here?" Jennifer asked. "One year to process and one year of mandatory separation," he answered. Tiffany shook her head. "Fuck no!" she responded firmly. Jennifer looked at Tiffany. "Do you want to spend the night here? I can watch Aidan," she asked. Tiffany looked at Jennifer surprised. "Would you?" she asked excitedly. Jennifer nodded, grabbing her clothes from the side of the bed, as Tiffany removed hers.

The next morning, David woke up, Tiffany holding onto him tightly. As he leaned to kiss her, she pulled him back on top of her. "What time is it?" she asked. "Just after seven am," he whispered. Pulling him close, she smiled. "We have time." Around 7:30, David and Tiffany went downstairs to find Jennifer feeding Aidan. "What's for breakfast big guy?" David asked. "Milk!" he responded. "He really is smart," he said. Tiffany nodded. "Just like his dad," she replied. David considered these words seriously as Jennifer handed Aiden off to get dressed for work.

Later that morning, David was able to call the family court in his hometown and even the next state they would be living. "So, what did you find out?" Tiffany asked. "We're going to have to hold off a bit. One of us has to be a resident for six months to file in Texas, and California requires six months of residence to file, but at least they don't have a separation period," he answered. Tiffany smiled. "We can wait then," she said as she played with Aidan. "Has it been difficult with Aidan by yourself?" he asked sincerely. "No, he's actually very well behaved for a baby. At first he was fussy, but while you were gone he was a lot easier to manage," she answered.

Two months later, everyone was celebrating Tiffany's 26th birthday. Jennifer, who had just turned 21 a month prior, wanted to celebrate her birthday with Tiffany. "Good morning sleepy head," David said as Jennifer came down the stairs. "Good morning Master," she responded playfully. "That always cracks me up," Tiffany said. "Have you thought about what you wanted to do for your birthday?" he asked. Jennifer smiled. "Yes, I want to go shopping," she replied bluntly. "I'll make you both a cake if you'd like," he proposed. "No, I don't feel like eating cake, plus I haven't been feeling well lately." She replied. Tiffany interjected. "You can make me a cake," she said happily.

The three ate breakfast as Aidan wandered around the dining room. "Shall we all go shopping together?" Tiffany suggested. "No, just us girls if that's okay." David didn't object, picking up Aidan. "You two have fun and I'll teach this one how to climb the stairs while you're gone," he smiled. "Don't let him get hurt," Tiffany exclaimed. True to his word, after Tiffany and Jennifer left, David immediately took Aidan to the bottom of the stairs and put him on the bottom step. After finally making it to the top, David continued to lay next to him as they came down the stairs.

After several hours, Jennifer entered the house and ran upstairs. As Tiffany walked through the door, David went to greet her. "Did you two have fun?" he asked. "I suppose so, but you'd have to ask Jennifer yourself," Tiffany responded. David thought for a moment before going upstairs to check on Jennifer. "Are you alright?" he asked, standing at the bathroom door. "I'm okay, I just really had to use the bathroom," Jennifer responded. David shrugged and went downstairs.

Several minutes later, Jennifer came downstairs. David was starting their cake as Tiffany read with Aidan on the couch. "Are you feeling better?" Tiffany asked, looking at Jennifer. "Yes, much better," she responded. Jennifer went into the kitchen. "Master, I got a present for you when we were at the store today," Jennifer said with a sly smile. "You didn't have to get me anything, it's not my birthday," he responded. Jennifer smiled as she held up a small box. "Let's wait until after you and Tiffany open your presents," he suggested. Jennifer smiled as she put the box on the table.

Later that evening, The four of them sat around the dining room table finishing dinner as David brought out the cake. Jennifer smiled. "I actually think I want cake now," she mumbled, staring at the cake. After the girls blew out the candles, everyone got a slice, including Aidan.

David pulled out the first present. "This was sent by Summer and it's for all of us," David said. Tiffany opened the wrapper, revealing a panoramic painting of the four of them at prom. "Can we put this in the living room?" Jennifer asked. "Sure," he responded. The next gift was from Tiffany to Jennifer. "I wanted to give this to you on your birthday," Tiffany said smiling. Jennifer opened the box to find matching sterling bracelets, with the word 'sisters' engraved on the plate. "What about Summer?" Jennifer asked. "I have one for her too," Tiffany answered.

David pulled out the next box. This one was for Tiffany from David. As she opened the box, she gasped. Is this what I think it is?" she asked excitedly. David nodded. Jennifer was confused, because Tiffany was holding a laminated business card. "What is it?" Jennifer asked. Tiffany handed the card to Jennifer who looked at it confused. "Is that a code or something?" she asked. "Yes, it's the code he writes his notes in, so now I can read it with this," she said, seemingly elated about something so simple. "It won't help you translate everything, but it should be a starting point," he said as Tiffany kissed him excitedly.

The next present was for Tiffany from Jennifer. As Tiffany opened the box, Jennifer bounced in her seat, seemingly more excited than Tiffany. Tiffany gasped as she opened the small box, lifting out a cameo with a woman's bust carved into sardonyx, set in a gold pennant inlaid with topaz. Tiffany started to cry as she held the pennant in her hand. "Do you like it?" Jennifer asked. Tiffany smiled. "I feel like this means so much more coming from you," she answered, still crying. Meanwhile, David was impressed but curious. "Who is the engraving of?" he asked. Jennifer attached the pennant to a velvet choker before answering. "It's Rhea, daughter of Gaia and mother of all the gods, also known as the great mother," Jennifer explained as she put the choker around Tiffany's neck.

The next present was for Jennifer from David. Jennifer looked side eyed at David, expecting something simple, like Tiffany's card, but when she opened the box, she squealed. As Jennifer pulled out a large metal ring, Tiffany furrowed her eyebrows. "What the hell is that?" Tiffany asked. "It's an eternity collar," he answered. Handing it to David, Jennifer immediately jumped up and knelt down, removing her choker. After David tightened the collar, Tiffany gasped. "Oh, now I see why she's so excited." After Jennifer stood up, she immediately grabbed the last box, handing it to David.

David set the box down and pulled the ribbon on top, as Tiffany and Jennifer watched. After opening the box, Tiffany gasped. "Is that what I think it is?" she asked in surprise. "It certainly looks like it," David said, still staring at the object in the box. "I'm going to have a baby!" Jennifer screamed excitedly. Tiffany hugged Jennifer, then Jennifer kissed David. Meanwhile, Aidan's face was half covered in chocolate at this point.

The following summer, David was at work when he received a call during the breakfast meal. "Sergeant Renado, your wife is on the phone, she said it's important," his supervisor said. David took the phone. "Hello. Uh huh. Right now? Okay, I'll let them know." After hanging up the phone, David turned to his sergeant. "Jennifer's going into labor, and I have to take her to the hospital." "Do what chu gotta do man. Do you have someone to watch the baby," he asked. "Yeah, my wife is home," he said as he turned around to leave. The staff sergeant thought for a moment. "Wait, who the hell is having a baby!? Who's Jennifer!?" the sergeant yelled as David walked out the door.

As David pulled up to the house, Jennifer was already waiting outside with Tiffany. "Good luck you two," Tiffany said as she shut the door after Jennifer. Despite her extreme state of pregnancy, Jennifer was actually calm. David figured she had either gotten pointers from Tiffany or was putting on a brave front. "Are you doing alright?" he asked, touching her hand. Jennifer nodded, "I'm ready to get this over with," she answered. "Are you planning on using baby formula or is my refrigerator going to be half titty milk?" he asked jokingly. Jennifer chuckled. "That really depends on how much I can get out of these milkers," she retorted, squeezing her own tits. David smiled, kissing her hand.

David had to purchase separate insurance for Jennifer, as it was impossible to claim her as a dependent with Tiffany being his wife and Jennifer being over 21. So rather than driving to the Military hospital, he went to the local hospital, just south of the base. There, Jennifer was taken upstairs while David filled out the paperwork. Once they got to the room, the doctor checked Jennifer out and immediately confirmed that she was dilated enough to be admitted. David chuckled. "What's so funny?" Jennifer asked, breathing heavily. "It's the admission form, I wrote your name as the patient and mother, my name as the father, and under emergency contact, I put Tiffany," he said, tapping the clipboard with the pen. "Well, that makes sense but how is that funny?" she asked. "Under relationship, should I write her relationship to you, or to me?" he asked. Jennifer grinned. "Put your relationship, I wanna see what they say," she said menacingly.

Several minutes later, a nurse walked in to catch David beatboxing while dancing like a robot to Jennifer's rhythmic breathing. David stopped, as Jennifer smiled at the nurse, still breathing rhythmically. "We've got you all checked in and your vitals are good, but I needed to clear up some information on the paperwork," she said, looking at the clipboard. David and Jennifer grinned at each other, then looked at the nurse. "What's the issue?" David asked. The nurse looked at Jennifer, who wouldn't break eye contact. "Is Tiffany your wife?" pointing at David. "Yes, that's correct," he replied. "But you're the father of this child?" she asked, hesitantly. "Yes, yes he is," Jennifer answered. "So, I thought maybe you were a surrogate, but you both have the same address and she's on your insurance policy," the nurse said, pointing with her pen. Jennifer smiled as she took a deep breath. "There's no mistake, I also belong to him," she said seriously. The nurse responded in a surprised tone, "Oh, well in that case, there's no questions, I'll just submit this as is."

David and Jennifer continued to goof around in the delivery room, even as he tended to her during her contractions. She was only in labor for three hours when his second son was born. "What is his name?" the doctor asked. "Brian," David replied. "You're quite fortunate young lady, your labor was considerably easier than most for your first child." Jennifer smiled as she held David's hand." "That's because my master has a huge cock," she said, as if it were nothing at all. The doctor stifled a laugh as David openly chuckled. The nurse, however, nearly fumbled the baby as she carried him to be cleaned.

"Am I going to be able to go home today?" she asked. "No, you'll have to stay overnight," the doctor replied. "Why is that?" she asked. David cleared his throat. "That's to let your body go back to the way it was. Otherwise, your organs that were pushed around during pregnancy, will just tumble around until it does, and that could be pretty uncomfortable," David said confidently. "Also, we still have to monitor you in case there are any complications," the nurse added. Jennifer frowned, "I liked his answer better," she said, rubbing David's arm. The nurse shook her head as she mumbled, "Of course you would."

That afternoon, Tiffany arrived with Aidan at the hospital to look after Jennifer while David went home to change out of his uniform. Jennifer held Brian as Tiffany lifted Aidan to meet his younger brother when the nurse walked into the room. "Oh, hello, you have company already?" she asked. Jennifer smiled. "Yes, this is Tiffany, David's wife." Tiffany waved Aidan's hand at the nurse. "You're his wife?" Tiffany nodded, "Uh huh." "And this is your son?" she asked, confused. "Yep, meeting his younger brother," Tiffany replied. "So, are you two related?" the nurse asked. Jennifer nudged Tiffany before responding, "Well, we are now." The nurse stared at the two women, as if her brain glitched, then turned to leave. "What was that about?" Tiffany asked. "We've been fucking with her all day," Jennifer answered.

When David returned, Aidan was eating Jennifer's fruit gelatin, as Jennifer was breastfeeding Brian. Meanwhile, Tiffany was watching the television in the room. "They haven't moved you to the mother-baby unit yet?" he asked. "No, they were waiting for a space to open up," Tiffany responded. David knelt down and tried to talk Aidan into giving him his gelatin when the nurse entered the room. "We have a room ready," she announced. Jennifer reached back and covered herself with a blanket as Tiffany stood up. David snapped, prompting Aidan to jump to his feet, immediately grabbing his finger at his side. As the nurse prepared the bed to move, David, Tiffany and Aidan waited in the hallway.

Together, the entire group moved down the hall until they reached the mother-baby unit. "I'm surprised you got your own room," Tiffany said as she looked around. "Did you have to share with someone?" Jennifer asked. "No, I got lucky, but they did have a second bed in there," she answered. "That's one of the benefits of using private insurance instead of Tricare," The nurse interjected. Tiffany looked at David. "What made you pick this hospital?" "Last time I was here, my ex-wife and I visited a fellow church member after she had her baby at this hospital," David said with a wry smile. "When did this happen?" Jennifer asked. David thought for a moment. "I actually think it was around this same time, because I remember having two children, plus it was warm outside." Tiffany scrutinized David. "Why does that amuse you?" she asked, noticing his smile. "It's just that, she was always sickly, and he was like three times her size at least, so I can't imagine it was an easy delivery." On the other side of the room, the nurse was on the verge of a migraine, trying to make sense of these people.

Tiffany left with Aidan when Jennifer received her dinner from the orderly, while David decided to stay until she finished eating. "Master, are you going to be able to take care of me once I get home, or do you have to go to work?" Jennifer asked with puppy dog eyes. "Don't worry, I get ten days of paternity leave, so I'll be home for a few weeks," he assured her. Jennifer smiled as she ate her food. David paced back and forth as he held Brian, telling him about his brothers and the days they were born.

That afternoon, as David arrived at home, Tiffany was folding laundry in the living room as Aidan played in the basket. "Do you need help?" he asked. "No, I've got it. How was Jennifer when you left?" she wondered. "Good, but sad to see me go," he said as he sat beside her. "Tiffany." "Yes?" she replied. "We're going to have to get a bigger vehicle, and we might have to consider getting rid of one of the ones we have," he said. Tiffany thought for a moment. "What about Jennifer, won't she need a car?" "Probably, but I doubt everyone will need one at the same time. Even now, it's unnecessary." After putting Aidan to bed that night, Tiffany got into bed with David and promptly fell asleep.

Jennifer was released from the hospital the next day, and the five stayed home together for the entire two weeks, other than the weekend they bought their new vehicle. David and Tiffany traded in her car and purchased a 12 passenger van for their growing family. Jennifer never did go back to work and over the next few months, they all packed and prepared to move. He would be assigned to the foreign language center in California for 15 months while learning Arabic, a language he was already proficient in. It would take them six days to drive there, but David planned to spend a week at home before driving the rest of the way, so he requested two weeks of travel time. Three days before departing, packers and movers packed their entire household, aside from the luggage they had set aside, then loaded everything onto a moving truck the next day. They left early in the morning, pulling David's car behind them.

Chapter 20

An Unexpected Visitor

They had been living in California for just over a month at this point. Neither Tiffany nor Jennifer got a job and had been staying home with the boys during the day. Because they only managed to get a three bedroom house, Brian and Aidan had to share a room. Meanwhile, Tiffany continued to share a room with David while Jennifer occupied the second bedroom, occasionally swapping for the night. Shortly after arriving, David met with the county clerk and was able to get a residency waiver for their divorce, due to his military status. However, because he and Tiffany had a child, they still had to wait the six month processing time.

It was late fall again and due to the recent move, nobody wanted to have a birthday celebration this year. However, David insisted they all celebrate together during the winter break, as a family. One night, Tiffany, Jennifer and David were sitting in the living room watching television, just after putting the boys to bed, when Tiffany put down the notebook she was reading. "David, can I ask you something about your notebooks?" Tiffany asked. "Sure, what do you want to know?" he responded. "Why did you never pursue us before? I mean, we're barely mentioned at all and according to this, you've had many relationships, so, what happened?" David took a deep breath before answering. "We never got that close, plus every relationship I've ever had only ended up destroying me, so I wasn't in a rush to be hurt again.

Looking back, I think it's because I allowed them to be who they were. Meanwhile, I was expected to be what they wanted." Jennifer chimed in, "We're mentioned in there? Where am I?"

David turned off the television and gave his attention to Jennifer and Tiffany. "I knew Summer first back in elementary school, we even hung out for a while since we both walked home, and lived close together. However, she got in a fight and when I tried to stand up for her, she took it out on me, probably blaming me for what happened, so I kept my distance, and convinced myself that we hated each other." "What happened with me?" Tiffany asked. "We were neighbors, just like you remembered, but you had your friends, and I had mine, plus I was always self-conscious, so once you and your friends started hanging out more, I just kept my distance until you left for college." "What about me?" Jennifer asked. "We met at your sister's apartment during the summer after graduation. I was staying there because I had been kicked out of my parents' house and my brother's friends took me in, hence your sister." "Were we friends?" she asked. "No, but they were trying to set us up, however, I was already 18 years old and leaving in a couple of months, so I had to decline. Plus, I was constantly surrounded by my ex, which made everything difficult."

"So, nothing ever happened?" they asked. David shook his head. "Summer got lucky this time, but I never knew you two well enough to really get involved, so we were able to start fresh. However, I was still apprehensive because my past relationships either destroyed my childhood, crippled my future, took everything I owned, or ruined my faith in relationships. All because I let them be who they were, and in the end, I had to distance myself as quickly as possible, so I left and never looked back." "What about the rest? Surely some of them must have been able to get close to you." David nodded. "They did, but something always pulled us apart or kept us apart. The worst is when they refuse to move because you're too good for them, or they're waiting for something that never happens."

Jennifer raised her hand. "I have a question." "What is it?" he asked. "If this is all about preparing for the end of the world, then why aren't you building an army or something?" she asked. David smiled at her before responding. "You mean why a harem of women?" "What's a harem?" Tiffany asked. "It's like when a guy has a house full of wives and concubines," he answered. Jennifer squinched her eyebrows. "Actually, I'd like to know both reasons," she said seriously. "Men will always want to lead, especially anyone capable of fighting, and we aren't going to war. So, what's the point in inviting such conflict. Plus, you aren't just concubines. I expect you all to contribute, for your life, for your children, and for me."

David continued to explain his rationale, talking into the night as it got late. Eventually, David took his women to bed, laying them side by side as he undressed them. Tiffany partially covered herself with the sheet as she waited for David while Jennifer sat with her legs crossed, wearing nothing but her collar. After getting into bed with them, he pulled the sheet covering Tiffany away and lifted her onto his lap. With her arms and legs wrapped around him, she pushed her hips hard into him, desperate to feel him inside of her. As he guided his cock in, she gasped, feeling every inch fill her up as she squeezed him tightly. Meanwhile, Jennifer seemed to be focused on Tiffany, standing on her knees right behind her as she kissed Tiffany's neck and shoulders.

After Tiffany came, he laid her down on the pillow, kissing her as she continued to hold him with her arms. David sat up once her legs relaxed and Jennifer cut in, as if she was trying to enter a line dance. David smiled and Tiffany looked at Jennifer shocked. Jennifer was looking down on top of Tiffany, almost like she was subbing in for David. David grabbed Tiffany's legs and pushed Jennifer's body down onto Tiffany, stacking the two on top of each other. As Jennifer looked back at him briefly, he immediately slid his cock inside of her, eliciting a heavy gasp, followed by a long moan. As David fucked Jennifer, Jennifer began making out with Tiffany. It didn't take long for Tiffany to start masturbating with David fucking Jennifer on top of her, but as soon as Jennifer came, David switched.

Jennifer never stopped kissing Tiffany, and Tiffany's body naturally responded. However, once David switched to Tiffany, she immediately took the lead, grabbing Jennifer and pulling her with every thrust David gave. David allowed the two to switch places after David eventually came inside of Tiffany, promising to fill Jennifer next. Of course, after a while, he relied on their feedback as he could no longer tell when they had finished. David eventually came inside of Jennifer, signaling the end to another sweaty and sex filled night.

The next morning, both women were acting much more submissive and compliant, something he noticed each time they were with him. After everyone showered, David went to the kitchen to make breakfast, Tiffany began washing the bedding from the night prior, and Jennifer tended to the boys. Aidan was eating solid food, so he eventually joined his father in the kitchen while Jennifer fed Brian in the living room. Aidan was already speaking in full sentences, so David insisted that everyone speak to him as if he were an equal member of the family, rather than an incapable child. Tiffany found this to be the most difficult, and still coddled him, which David noticed, but allowed.

The following month, classes were being released for the holidays and rather than having to go into work for no reason, David requested leave as well. At home, everyone found it difficult to get into the holiday spirit because of David's strict adherence to the budget and the unchanging weather on the west coast. However, this didn't stop Tiffany from trying to stir things up. "David, I know you don't want us getting involved with the FRG, but what do you think about having a Christmas party with your classmates before the holidays?" she asked. "Sure, but are we going to have it here?" he asked. "We'll keep it simple if that's an issue for you," she reassured him. David accepted and went to tell Jennifer, who immediately came running to Tiffany, like a girl being invited to Disney land.

The next afternoon in class, David raised his hand. "ladaya 'iielanu. eayilati satuqim haflat eid almilad al'usbue almuqbil watarghab zawjati fi hudurikum jmyean 'iidha kuntum mutahina." His instructor's smiled as his classmates struggled to understand his announcement. They had only been in class for two months and were not that proficient. After looking at the confused looks of his classmates, he looked to his instructor, who nodded his head. "My family is having a Christmas party next week and my wife would like all of you to come, if you are free," he said.

Suddenly hit with realization, his classmates began to talk amongst themselves.

That afternoon, before leaving class, his department head summoned him to his office. As he waited outside the door, Sergeant First Class Michael Villa approached him. Sergeant Villa was his MPI, or military proficiency instructor, serving as a liaison to the students on behalf of the instructor cadre, which were all civilians. "Sergeant Villa, can you tell me why we're here?" David asked. "It's not bad, if that's what you're worried about, but Mr. Farid heard about your announcement today." "I'm not planning on letting the initial entry trainees visit, if that's the problem," David said, waving his hands. "I wouldn't worry about that, he just wants to talk," he reassured him. After David and Sergeant Villa were called in, Mr. Farid asked them to sit and offered them a drink.

David declined and asked. "limadha talabt ruyati alyawma?" "kunt mujarad fuduli, 'ayn taealamt altahaduth biallughat alearabiati?" he asked. "laqad taealamt dhalik mundh waqt tawili, lakin la 'astatie 'an 'ukhbirak mataa 'aw kayfa," David answered. Mr. Farid nodded his head. "'ana 'afham dhalika, walakin limadha la taqum bi'iijra' aliakhtibaru, walimadha tati 'iilaa huna 'iidha kunt tuerifuh bialfieli?" "li'ana majiyiy 'iilaa hadhih almadrasat kan shyyan kan lzaman ely fielah, wamil 'alaa yuathir hadha ealaa waqti huna katalibatin." David said with a serious expression. "rubama yakun hadha sirna alsaghira," he said, smiling.

David declined and asked. "Why did you ask to see me today?" "I was just curious, where did you learn to speak Arabic?" he asked. "I learned a long time ago, but I can't tell you when or how," David answered. Mr.

Farid nodded his head. "I understand, but why not just take the test, why come here if you already know?" "Because coming here to this school was something I had to do, and I hope this doesn't affect my time here as a student," David said with a serious expression. "It can be our little secret," he said smiling.

David walked in the house, immediately greeted by Aidan, then subsequently by Tiffany. "Did you tell them?" she asked, standing on her tiptoes. "Yes, but I may have caused a bit of trouble in the process." Tiffany stepped back. "Did I get you in trouble?" she asked. "No, but they might have found out that I'm more proficient than they were led to believe," he answered as he removed his uniform top. "Go see Jennifer, I'll take care of dinner today," she said as she kissed him on the cheek. David walked into Jennifer's room as she was feeding Brian. "You wanted to see me?" "Yes, I wanted to ask you something before I lost my nerve," she said hesitantly. "Just say it then," he said as he sat down. Jennifer took a deep breath and closed her eyes. "Tiffany and I were talking, and she told me why she wanted a divorce. Apparently you had an agreement, and I wanted to ask before Summer got here," Jennifer spoke softly as she obviously avoided the question. "Out with it," he demanded. "I wanted to know if you would marry me next," she said in a single breath.

David smiled as he stood up. "I thought you were content just being my pet," he asked. "Yes Master, I am. But I also wanted, you know." Jennifer stumbled over her words as David smiled down at her. "Don't worry so much about saying the right thing, I promised your mother, so we can get married." Jennifer smiled. "When?" she asked, looking up at him. David pondered for a moment. "How about right after we pick up our divorce papers." Jennifer laughed. "That would be so funny!" she exclaimed. As Jennifer went to share the news with Tiffany, David took a shower.

After getting out of the shower, he was in his room getting dressed as he heard a commotion coming from the living room. David left his room, following the sounds of the voices when he suddenly saw a face he wasn't expecting. "Sergeant McKean, what are you doing here?" he asked. "I actually live up the street and I wanted to stop by after your invitation today," she answered. "You don't have anyone at home?" he asked. She hung her head. "No, my husband's out playing games, apparently, that's what he wants to do with his life now," she said resentfully. David knew this all too well, Sergeant Elena McKean was in a dysfunctional marriage with a former soldier, and even though she was attending language school, had no intention of graduating, but simply wanted to finish her military contract without deploying.

"Well, we're about to eat dinner and apparently, we have a party to plan for," he said as he looked at Tiffany. "It's okay, I'll just go," she said, turning toward the door. "Wait, why don't you stay for dinner," Tiffany suggested. "No, it's okay." "No, there isn't anyone there anyway," Jennifer chimed in. David shrugged his shoulders at Elena, who smiled reluctantly. "If it's okay with you," she said. "It's fine by me," he assured her. As Jennifer walked her to the living room, David leaned close to Tiffany. "What do you have up your sleeve woman?" he asked. Tiffany smiled as she kissed him. "Go tend to our guest sir."

"So, do you both live here with Sergeant Renado?" Elena asked. "Yes, he takes care of us, but please, can you call him

David here?" Jennifer pleaded. "Sure, no problem," she agreed. David sat on the couch, watching the two talking when Aidan came walking into the room. "Dad, can I dig a hole?" David picked him up. "I'll let you dig a hole later, okay buddy?" David answered as he set him on his lap. "He talks really well, how old is he?" Elena asked. "He'll be three in the summer," David said dismissively. Elena was shocked, even though she didn't have children herself, even this seemed far-fetched. "Why does he want to dig a hole?" Jennifer asked. "He probably had a dream about it," David answered as he put him on the ground. Aidan ran back to his room as they continued their conversation.

"Dinner's ready!" Tiffany announced. As David and Elena joined Tiffany at the table, Jennifer went to get Brian and Aidan came running, climbing into his booster seat. "This looks really good," Elena exclaimed. "Thank you, David taught me how to make it," Tiffany said, smiling. Jennifer set Brian in a highchair and handed him a bowl of mashed food. As everyone else began filling their plates. Elena watched everyone's interactions as she slowly ate her food. "Can I ask you guys a question?" "Sure, go ahead," Tiffany responded as she put food on Aidan's plate. "I know you're his wife, but how is everybody else related?" she asked, pointing at Jennifer. "Oh, we're actually getting a divorce, so, soon I'll be his ex-wife." Elena nearly choked on her food. "I don't understand!" David continued eating, never bothering to comment, but occasionally glanced at the others. "And I'm getting married soon," Jennifer announced proudly.

Elena never bothered to follow up, but couldn't help but notice Jennifer's gaze. "You are really pretty," Jennifer told Elena. "Thank you, I guess." Elena blushed as she pulled her hair behind her ear. 'Master, where do you think she's from?" Jennifer asked. Elena nearly choked again at her words. "She's half Korean and I believe half native?" he guessed, looking at Elena. She nodded her head. "Navajo," she answered, food still in her mouth. "So, either New Mexico or Arizona," he said, looking at her again. Elena's face nearly froze at his accuracy. "Tucson," she clarified. David nodded, going back to his dinner. Tiffany smiled as she ate her food, watching the other three's interaction.

After dinner, Elena prepared to go home. "Will you come back and visit again?" Jennifer asked as she walked Elena to the door. "We'll see, but I'll definitely come to the party," she said as she opened the door. Jennifer hugged Elena, surprising her as she prepared to leave. "You don't have to bring your husband," Jennifer whispered. After closing the door, Jennifer grabbed Brian and Joined David on the couch as Tiffany washed the dishes. "We should go buy presents this weekend," she suggested. "Sure, that sounds like a good idea, but I wouldn't know what to get, and I don't know who's all coming," he said. Tiffany walked into the living room after finishing the dishes and grabbed Brian from Jennifer before kissing David. "I'm going to get these guys in the bathtub, you two enjoy your moment," Tiffany said as she gestured for Aidan to follow.

David and Jennifer continued discussing their ideas as Tiffany bathed the boys, eventually putting them to bed. As she returned to the living room, she gasped sarcastically. "Jennifer, I'm surprised you still have your clothes on," she joked. Jennifer rolled her eyes as she stood, heading to the bathroom. "What are you thinking," he asked, curious about her intentions. Tiffany smiled. "I remember seeing her name in your book, so when she came by, I wanted to see what kind of person she was." David smiled, patting her on the head. "You are a remarkable woman," he said as she blushed profusely. Tiffany took a shower after Jennifer and everyone went to bed.

That weekend, Tiffany and Jennifer went shopping as David stayed home playing with his boys. He purchased an above ground pool for Aidan's second birthday, along with several hundred pit balls. After setting up his ball pit, he threw Aidan in and held Brian as he stepped inside the pit. For the next four hours, Aidan would jump and swim in the pit as Brian grabbed whatever balls he could reach, laughing at Aidan as he jumped around like a whale breaching. Meanwhile, Tiffany and Jennifer got to enjoy their shopping trip without David's systematic and robot like behavior.

Late in the afternoon, Tiffany and Jennifer arrived and David was on his computer, working on his timeline. "Where are the boys?" Tiffany asked. Without looking up, David responded. "They worked hard today, so they're both taking a nap." Jennifer went to their room to check and sure enough, they were both fast asleep. "You know Master, it's okay to let them play once in a while," she said as she shut the door. David closed his work and stood up to greet them. "Did you two have fun at the store?" he asked. "We did, we even went to the mall. Did you know the mall here is all outdoors?" she said excitedly. David smiled. "Never mind, of course you know," she sighed.

Over the next few days, Tiffany and Jennifer prepared for their Christmas party as David wrapped the presents and even took his boys to the beach. The day before the party, someone knocked on their door. Jennifer answered the door and gasped.

"Summer! You made it!" Summer hugged Jennifer as Tiffany came running. "Did you just get here?" Summer sighed, carrying her bag. "Yes, I had no idea how long this trip would be when I left though. Did you know the valley is so foggy that you can't even see through it?" Summer asked. "It wasn't foggy when we came through it, but maybe David knows," Tiffany responded while grabbing her bags. "How was school, are you a doctor now?" Jennifer asked excitedly. Summer sighed as she plopped on the couch, exhausted. "Yes, I'm a doctor of pharmacy now, and not a moment too soon."

Summer looked around, "Where's David?" Jennifer took Summer's bag to her room. "He took the boys to the beach," Tiffany answered. Summer sat up, confused. "Boys? You mean Aidan and the baby?" "Yep," Jennifer responded as she walked back to the living room. "He probably has them digging trenches or storming the dunes like Normandy. Summer smiled, "I think we should go surprise him." In less than ten minutes, Summer's car was filled with curious women on a mission. Within fifteen minutes, Summer parked, and the three ladies stepped out. "It's the middle of December, why does it feel like spring here," Summer asked. "It's like this all year apparently, but the water is freezing cold," Tiffany responded.

As the three walked down the beach searching for David, they marveled at the ocean and its vast expanse. "The waves are smaller here," Summer exclaimed. "Yeah, I thought the same thing," Tiffany answered. As they got further down the beach, they could make out the silhouette of a man and two children, flying kites. "There he is!" Summer yelled as she took off running. "Looks like they forgot their shovels," Tiffany quipped, poking

Jennifer in the arm. Jennifer didn't respond, but stared at the sight in front of her. Watching him flying kites with his children at the beach nearly made her uterus skip a beat.

Chapter 21

The Portrait of Venus

Tiffany and Jennifer were getting ready for the Christmas party that evening when Summer walked into the room. "Is there anything I can help with?" she asked. Not stopping their work, Tiffany responded. "It's okay, you just got here yesterday, leave this to us. Besides, I think you have some catching up to do." Summer wasn't about to argue and went out to the back yard where David was helping Aidan throw a collapsable hamper full of pit balls into another hamper. "It's fascinating how such a simple toy can be so entertaining for a child," Summer said as she smiled. "It's also fascinating how such a simple game can have such implications on a person's growth," David responded. "Did you have pit balls before?" she asked as she watched. "Yes, we had them for years. When they got older, we used them like snowballs in a snowball fight," he said.

Summer sat in a chair admiring the sight in front of her. Aidan would miss half the shots he took, but David continued to encourage him. Meanwhile, Brian was crawling around, retrieving the pit balls and bringing them to his father, often ending in some kind of praise. "Have you considered getting a dog? I heard taking care of a dog might help young boys learn responsibility," Summer asked. David thought for a moment. "Actually, I have. Aidan definitely wants a dog, and I miss having a roving vacuum cleaner," he joked.

Summer sat in silence for a few moments before her tone became serious. "How has your planning been going?" she asked. David hesitated before answering. "I'm a little concerned about money, but I've started investing, so hopefully, we'll have enough." "I don't suppose you know what stocks are going to blow up, do you?" David shook his head. "I had no reason to, so I just picked one I knew would do well, hopefully it works out," he replied dismissively. Summer was genuinely curious. Leaning forward, she asked. "Which one?" David stopped as he turned to face her. "Apple." Summer was genuinely shocked. "The computer company?" she asked, doubt in her voice. Apple had only just released iTunes, and their iPod was still new. "Give it time," David reassured her. "How much money do you have now?" she asked. David paused before answering. "Probably close to half a million," he said like it was nothing. "Jesus Christ! How much do you need?" she gasped. "Millions."

As the sun started going down, Tiffany and Jennifer were already set up, and Brian was taking a nap as several of David's classmates began to show up. The first to arrive was Staff Sergeant Jared Smith, a Marine Corps analyst and avid surfer along with his wife Megan. David talked with Jared as Megan talked with the other women, relieved to be amongst like-minded peers. Megan was a country girl, so she connected more with Tiffany and the two seemed inseparable from the moment she arrived. Within the next hour, Sergeant Michael Villa arrived alone, alongside Senior Airman Julian Weeks with his wife Courtney, a pretentious rich chick from New York. Michael was impressed by the set up and complimented David on his home, however, David immediately gave credit to his wife Tiffany and Jennifer for the decorations.

David saw Summer talking with Courtney, who clearly had a stick up her ass, while her husband Julian seemed determined to elevate his own social standing, something David felt was a response to his wife's insatiable lust for material things. Michael and Jared had settled on the couch next to Aidan, looking for something to watch on the television. Meanwhile Tiffany continued chatting with Megan as Jennifer topped off the food and beverages. David watched as his guests settled in. While the women sat at the table talking, the men sat on the couch, watching the Portland Trailblazers play the Chicago Bulls. Just then, the doorbell rang.

Jennifer answered the door and responded excitedly. "Elena, you made it!" Elena embraced Jennifer and the two walked into the dining room side by side, followed by her husband Ryan, who felt out of place and dressed like a teenager in an adult's body. Elena was welcomed by Tiffany warmly, who hugged her and offered her a drink. Ryan sat in the living room with the rest of the men, but didn't say a word, meanwhile, Summer joined Tiffany at the table with Jennifer, Megan and Elena, after Courtney had convinced her husband to leave early. David saw them out and thanked Julian for coming before returning to the living room.

While they watched the game, David, Michael and Jared talked about their careers and experiences as the women talked about their husbands, hobbies and the latest gossip. Even though Elena felt out of place amongst the women, her reception and friendliness of the other women made her feel comfortable and at ease. Meanwhile, Ryan obviously didn't want to be there, despite several attempts to bring him in on the conversation. Everyone knew that Tiffany was David's wife, so naturally, they just assumed that Summer and Jennifer were a part of her social circle.

David invited Summer and Elena to join their conversation, as their military backgrounds might add a different perspective to the group. "How do you know David?" Michael asked. Summer smiled as she looked at David. "David and I kinda grew up together." The group quietly talked amongst themselves for a moment. "What was David like back then?" Elena asked, hoping to get some dirt on him. Summer thought before responding. "Actually, he was the same as he is now, but I like him more now than I did then," she said mischievously. "How do you know Tiffany and Jennifer," Elena asked. "Through David I guess. Jennifer and I became friends in high school, but I met Tiffany just before graduation," she responded. "Wait, you've all known each other that long?" Jared asked, surprised. "Uh huh," Summer nodded her head.

As David and Michael stepped outside for a moment, Elena joined Summer in the kitchen to get a drink, while Jennifer was returning from checking on Brian as she was intercepted by Ryan in the hallway. "I haven't seen you drinking the whole night, isn't this your party too?" he asked. "I have to take care of the baby, so I can't drink, but this is Tiffany's party, not mine," she responded coldly. As Jennifer started walking toward the kitchen, Ryan grabbed her arm. "Maybe if you get a break, you could come watch me play in a tournament sometime," he suggested. Jennifer smiled, sensing his intent. "What kind of tournament?" she asked, leaning against the wall. "I'm a pro gamer, and we have a Madden tournament coming up next year, you know, if you're interested," he said.

Summer handed Elena a drink from the refrigerator. "So, you were in the reserves?" Elena asked. "Yes, as a pharmacy technician. But I finished my contract six months ago," Summer responded. "What are you going to do now?" Summer smiled. "I just got my Doctor of Pharmacy degree, so I'm going to look for a job next year. Why?" Elena lowered her head. "I plan on getting out soon and I was just wondering what I should do," she responded, uncertainty in her voice. "What about your husband?" Summer asked. Elena let out a deep sigh. "He's a piece of shit. He thinks he can become a professional gamer, but I'm the one that ends up paying for everything," she replied. "Why don't you just divorce him?" Summer suggested. Elena sighed. "I will, I just haven't decided when."

As David and Michael came back in the house, Tiffany stood up. "Alright everyone, time to pass out presents." Jared and Megan looked at Michael. "We were supposed to bring presents?" Michael shrugged his shoulders. "So, we should decide who gets the first present," Tiffany announced, as she laid out boxes on the table. Elena raised her hand. "I didn't bring anything," she said nervously. Jennifer and Tiffany smiled. "You didn't have to," they both responded. Twelve boxes of equal size were laid out on the dining room table without names or labels. "The rule is, one person open's the gift, and the next person in line can either steel the gift or take a new one. If your gift is stolen, you have to open a new one. But you have to open it as soon as you pick it up." Tiffany explained. "You mean like dirty Santa?" Jared asked. "Exactly," David answered.

"I think that we should allow them to pick based on order of arrival, the last goes first," David suggested. Everyone agreed, as Ryan stepped forward to pick the first gift. After unwrapping the box, he removed a red beanie, made to look like a big cherry. Jennifer laughed. "Now you can be all that with a cherry on top," she joked. Ryan smiled politely as he put the cherry beanie back into the box. Elena stepped forward and grabbed another box. After unwrapping the box, she revealed a package of whiskey stones. "What the hell are these?" she asked, reading the package. "They're used like ice cubes for alcohol," David said, arms crossed. Michael grabbed a third box and opened it, revealing an unscented candle. Pleased with his gift, he smiled. Jared stepped forward and took the unscented candle from Michael, who sadly took another box from the table. After unwrapping this box, he pulled out a magic eight ball.

Tiffany smiled when she saw this. "Ask it a question," she said, still smiling. Michael closed his eyes for a moment, then rolled the eight ball. After reading the answer he tried it three more times, his smile widening more each time. Jared looked curiously at the eight ball as Megan reached for a new box. After opening the box, she pulled out a clit vibrator. Megan's eyes widened as she shoved it back into the box. Jennifer raised her hand. "My turn!" eliciting sudden groans from the group. However, to everyone's surprise, she took Elena's whiskey stones. David watched her curiously as she smiled at Elena, who was all too happy to pick a different gift. As Elena approached the table, Jennifer watched expectantly as she reached for another box. Satisfied with her choice, Elena opened the box, revealing a bottle of intense arousal serum. "What's this?" she asked. Jennifer smiled, "I'll show you later," she said as she winked. After clapping her hands, Tiffany concluded the gift exchange.

"What's so funny about that magic eight ball?" Jared asked Michael. "Look, it doesn't matter what question you ask, all the answers are no," he replied smiling. Ryan waited by the door, ready to leave as Jennifer escorted Elena to the bathroom. Meanwhile, Jared and Megan told David and Tiffany goodnight, thanking them for the evening. Summer hugged Megan and as they left, Elena emerged from the bathroom, blushing with an eerie smile on her face. Michael thanked David and left shortly after Jared and Megan. As Elena and Jennifer continued talking, Ryan sighed audibly. Frustrated at his impatience, Elena took Ryan outside.

Aidan was still sitting on the couch, watching a movie as the room began to clear out. "Ready for a bath little buddy?" David asked as he picked him up, carrying him to the bathroom. Jennifer got Brian from his room and brought him to the bathroom as well. Summer was helping Tiffany clear the table as Jennifer entered the kitchen. "I don't think Ryan fucks his wife," Jennifer whispered. Summer stopped, looking at Jennifer. "How do you know?" Summer asked. "I can tell, plus, I think he was hitting on me earlier." Tiffany rushed over. "What did you do?" she asked in a serious tone. Jennifer wore a devilish smile. "I just played along for now." Summer turned to Tiffany. "Tiffany, is it okay if I sleep with David tonight?" Tiffany responded quickly. "Sure, I don't mind," returning to her work. "Ahem, Sorry, I should have said something," Elena said, standing at the door. Jennifer rushed over, hugging Elena.

"I thought you were going home!" Jennifer exclaimed, bringing Elena to the table. "No, he just wanted to go play video games and I didn't want to sit and watch," she responded quietly. Summer brought Elena another drink as Elena sat deep in thought. "Is it true?" she asked. Jennifer and Summer looked at each other. "Yes," Jennifer responded. Elena sighed. "I figured. Where's David?" Elena asked. "He's washing the boys in the bathtub," Tiffany answered. Elena kept staring at her bottle, deciding how to approach the topic. "Summer, why do you want to sleep with David?" she asked. Summer smiled, showing no semblance of embarrassment. "Because I love him." The entire room suddenly became heavy with silence, even Tiffany stopped cleaning.

"But he's married, and he even has a son. How can you say that in front of his wife?" Elena asked seriously. Jennifer chuckled. "Technically, he has two sons." Elena looked at Tiffany. "You have two sons?" Tiffany shook her head. "Brian is my son," Jennifer interjected. Elena's head began to spin. "So, the other day, when you called him Master, I wasn't hearing things?" Elena asked, exasperated. Jennifer shook her head. Tiffany took a book off the shelf and removed a picture she had been using as a bookmark. Placing it in front of Elena. As Elena examined the picture of the four of them at prom, Tiffany said sincerely. "We all belong to him."

Despite Elena's confusion, she didn't want to leave, finding the whole situation amusing, even though she had only known them for a brief time, her relationship with Tiffany and

Jennifer gave her a familial sense of comfort. "How old is David?" Elena asked. "Twenty four," Summer answered. "And you're all the same age?" Tiffany shook her head. "I'm twenty seven and Jennifer is twenty two." Elena smiled. "I want to hear all about this," she said, taking another drink.

David eventually took the boys out of the tub with Jennifer's help, as the rest of the women continued to chat in the dining room. Jennifer returned with Brian as David put Aidan to bed, returning to the group as well. "What are you wicked women scheming in my absence?" he said as he sat down. Summer smiled. "Girl talk," she said as the other's laughed. Elena was clearly tipsy, and Tiffany was staring at David while Summer leaned her head against him. "You must feel really special, having three women take care of you," Elena slurred. "It must have been really difficult to convince all of them to agree to this," she added, resting her chin on her arm. David nodded his head. "Indeed, it was."

As the night continued to pass, Jennifer eventually walked Elena home as Tiffany and Summer prepared for bed. Meanwhile, David put Brian to bed and took a shower. As he stepped out of the shower, Jennifer met him in the hallway. "Thank you for letting us have a party Master," she said as she kissed him. "Goodnight Jennifer," he responded as he ruffled her hair. As he entered his room, Summer waited wearing nothing but her silver choker. "Here he is, lord David and his army of concubines," Summer said smiling. David rolled his eyes. "Keep that shit up and you'll be sleeping with the rest," he said as he climbed into bed. Summer made a pouting face. "I was only kidding, besides, I like our little family." David kissed her as she rolled herself on top of him, turning out the bedside light.

That next weekend, everyone woke up early. Summer was making breakfast and Jennifer fed Brian on the couch while Tiffany made coffee. David walked into the living room, kissing Jennifer, then Brian on his forehead. Heading into the kitchen, he stopped Summer, kissing her as she held a spatula in her hand before kissing Tiffany while grabbing a coffee cup. "I have good news for everyone," he announced. Jennifer poked her head around the corner as Summer continued with her cooking, meanwhile, Tiffany just smiled wide eyed as she stared at him. "I'm going to be promoted at the beginning of the year," he said, suddenly feeling self-conscious under their gaze. Jennifer was excited at the news, but Tiffany had already learned this by reading his notebooks. Summer, on the other hand, didn't respond.

"What's the matter Summer?" he asked. Summer shook her head "It's fine, you probably deserve it." David wrapped his arms around her. "I don't know why you would be upset, after all, aren't you a certified pharmacist now?" he asked, teasing her. Summer smiled as she finished breakfast. As breakfast was being placed on the table, Aidan came running, wearing long sleeves and boots. "Where do you think you're going?" David asked. Without looking up, he simply responded, "I'm going to dig that hole!" Summer and Jennifer seemed amused by his persistence, but Tiffany only looked at David curiously. "I told you Aidan, not yet. Wait until Brian can walk, Okay?" Aidan hung his head, "Okay," he conceded.

After breakfast, everyone gathered in the living room next to the Christmas tree, as David sat on the floor. David marveled at their excitement as he started to pull out the packages one at a time. "Let's give Aidan the first present." David suggested, handing him a large box. As Aidan opened the box, Tiffany looked at David in disbelief. "You got him Legos?" David smiled. "Not just any Legos, the Millenium Falcon!" he exclaimed. "How is he supposed to put that together?" she asked, furrowing her eyebrow. "One piece at a time," David responded with a smile. Aidan picked up the box and immediately carried it to his room, as Summer and Jennifer stared amazed. "He's strong for a little guy," Jennifer said, still in disbelief.

David pulled out the next package. "This one is for Jennifer from Summer," he said, handing the present to Jennifer. As she removed the wrapper, she smiled, turning it to show everyone. Summer had painted a portrait of Jennifer as she saw her in the nursery. Wearing her coveralls while taking care of the plants. Jennifer leaned over to hug Summer, but kissed her before Summer could pull away. Tiffany smiled as David reached for another gift. "This one is for Tiffany from me," he said as he handed it to her. Tiffany opened the wrapping excitedly. "Where did you get this!" she exclaimed. Summer and Jennifer jumped at her sudden reaction. "What is it?" Jennifer asked. Tiffany pulled a long red dress out of the box. "It's the dress I wore to prom!" she said, holding it against her body. David smiled. "Actually, I bought the dress after you returned it," he responded.

David pulled out the next gift. "This one is for Summer from Jennifer." Summer opened the box revealing a sorted box of seeds, which included Asian Ginseng, Echinacea, Anise

Hyssop, Calendula, Ashwagandha, and Feverfew. Summer smiled as she looked through the box. "Don't worry, I'll help you grow them," Jennifer assured her. "The next present is for Summer from Tiffany." As Summer opened the small box, revealing a small metal bracelet, she couldn't help but notice the exact same bracelets on Tiffany and Jennifer's wrists. "Have you been waiting to give me this the whole time?" she asked. Tiffany nodded as Summer lunged at her.

David smiled as he pulled out the next gift. "This one is for me? Thank you Jennifer." David chuckled as he opened the box. "My Master is a sadist," David read as he held up a coffee mug. "I'm going to use this all the time." He said as he took the mug out of the box. Reaching for the next gift. "This one is for Tiffany from Summer." Tiffany laughed as she removed the wrapper. "I hope you like it," Summer said. Tiffany revealed the painting, causing everyone to chuckle. It was a rendition of the birth of Venus, but David, Summer and Jennifer's likenesses were surrounding Tiffany as she stood on the shell. "This is hilarious," Tiffany said as she set the painting aside.

"The next gift is for Summer from me," David said as he handed her the present. Summer opened the package, pulling out a medium sized wooden box. "What's this for?" she asked. "Open it," David said. As she opened the wooden box, she studied it's contents. "It's an apothecary box," she said, as she examined it. David nodded his head. Reaching for the next gift. "This one is for me from Summer." Summer smiled as he removed the wrapping. David was in shock as he looked in the box. "Do you not like it?" Summer asked as she noticed the smile disappear from his face. He shook his head. "No, I do, I'm just thinking about how to use it," he said seriously. "What did you get?" Jennifer asked, trying to peek. David lifted out a double sided massage wand, causing Tiffany to blush and Jennifer to gasp in surprise. David jumped to his feet suddenly and ran to his room.

After returning, he grabbed the next gift. "This one is for Jennifer from me," handing the present to Jennifer. "What did you do with the toy?" Jennifer asked. "I went to plug it in, now open your present," he demanded dismissively. Jennifer removed the wrapping and pulled out a small box. "An iPod?" David nodded. "Since you like listening to music as much as I do, I thought this would be a good idea," he said casually. "Will you show me how to use it?" she asked excitedly. Rather than answering, he leaned over and kissed her on the cheek. As David reached for the next present, Jennifer started bouncing in her seat. "The next present is for me from Tiffany," he said as Jennifer suddenly settled down. As David opened the box, he took out a large book. "What is this?" he asked, examining it's cover.

As he opened the book, he immediately recognized the writing inside, it was his own code, printed on every page. "You had my books published?" he asked. Tiffany shook her head. "No, I only had your memory books printed, and this is the only copy," she said as she smiled. David admired the embossed cover and parchment colored pages. "This is an amazing gift," he responded sincerely. "Get the last one!" Jennifer cried out, nearly jumping out of her skin. Without saying a word, David handed the last box to Tiffany, looking at Jennifer the entire time. Tiffany squinched her eyes as she pulled out a dysfunctional looking sex toy. "What is this for?" she asked, examining the object in her hand. "Remember that time when Master made us a sandwich?" Jennifer blurted. "I got it, you don't have to say it," Tiffany interrupted as she put the toy back in the box. Summer was confused, as if missing the punch line.

The rest of the day was pretty standard, with David helping Aidan build his Millennium Falcon and Brian blissfully playing with the empty boxes. Later that afternoon, they all ate a Christmas meal together talking about their plans for the new year.

Chapter 22

The Contributions We Make

Several months into the spring, David had just had his birthday, and everybody was getting dressed to go to court. Jennifer, now three months pregnant with her second child, invited Elena over to help. "Today's the big day? What is it you need help with?" Elena asked. As Tiffany grabbed her clutch, she turned toward her. "We need two witnesses to accompany us to the courthouse, so we wanted to ask if you could either watch the boys or come along with us." Elena was confused. "I get to choose?" she asked, looking at the two boys playing on the floor. Summer nodded. "I can stay here if you decide to go, if that's what you want." David didn't waste time. "Everybody into the van!" he commanded. Elena, with her proclivity for drama, decided to accompany the rest to the courthouse.

As the four exited the van, David led the group into the building. "Mister and Miss Renado for Judge Kingsley," he announced to the clerk. "It'll be just ten minutes, please have a seat in the waiting area." David escorted the women to the waiting area, sitting between Tiffany and Jennifer as Elena looked on with interest. After several minutes, the door opened. "Renado?" Nodding his head, David stood, leading the rest into the courtroom. Elena and Jennifer sat behind David and Tiffany respectively, as the judge looked through his paperwork.

"So, you're here today to finalize the dissolution of your marriage to David Renado?" the judge confirmed. Tiffany stood.

"Yes I am." "I see you already have a parenting plan and you two have agreed to handle the matter internally. Do you have a place to stay Miss Renado?" Tiffany looked at David. "Yes I do." Elena was stifling her laughter as Jennifer watched teary eyed. "I must say, this has been an easy process, and it's good to see two people handle such a thing with such maturity and civility, but before I sign this, I only have one question," the judge asked, taking off his glasses. David and Tiffany stared intently, not saying a word. "Why would you two want to get a divorce?" he asked. Tiffany stood, taking a deep breath. "Because my lesbian lover is pregnant with his child," she answered boldly.

Elena snorted as the judge stared dumbfounded while Jennifer approached Tiffany, kissing her in front of everyone. David shrugged as he stood up, thanking the judge for his time. As the four left the courtroom, David went back to the clerk. "Mister Renado and Miss Clarke for the deputy commissioner." The same clerk sighed as she checked her records. "Yes sir, just wait over there, he'll be with you in about forty minutes." Elena and Jennifer sat down as Tiffany and David stepped outside. "How are you feeling?" David asked, handing Tiffany a cigarette. Tiffany smiled as she lit her cigarette. "A lot has changed in the past ten years, but I wouldn't change any of it." David furrowed his eyebrow. "Any of it?" he asked, unconvinced. Tiffany leaned close to his ear. "I would have fucked you the first time I brought you home," she whispered.

After going back inside, Jennifer looked up at them. "I thought you two went to bang one out in the van," she joked. As they waited, Elena moved closer. "So, are you going to marry Summer too?" David looked at Jennifer before answering. "Yes,

If that's what she wants." Elena leaned back in her chair. "I don't know how you manage to keep three women so content and my husband can't even take care of one." Jennifer grabbed Elena's hand, not saying a word. Tiffany sat in contemplation for a few minutes before speaking. "I don't think it's ever that easy. After all, David's value came at a significant cost and while he bears that burden, we all benefit from it." Elena hung her head. "I wish I had your confidence," she mumbled. Tiffany leaned close to Elena. "I would worship David if he allowed it," she whispered. Tiffany's comment shocked Elena into complete silence.

Just then, the clerk called out. "Mister Renado and Miss Clarke, the Deputy Commissioner will see you now. Together, the four of them stood and walked toward his office, filing in one by one as David and Jennifer sat in the chairs in front of his desk. "So, you two are here to get married?" he asked. "Yes sir," David confirmed. "Do you have a driver's license or other ID?" After placing their licenses on the desk, he nodded. "According to this, you are currently applying for a dissolution of marriage from Miss Tiffany Renado?" he asked. David placed the divorce decree on the desk. "Okay, all I need from you now is the one hundred dollars for the processing fee, your name change request and two witnesses." David placed the money on the desk as Jennifer put her name change form next to it. After signing the document, David and Jennifer stepped aside as Tiffany and Elena signed the witness blocks.

The Deputy Commissioner looked at the paperwork, then up at Tiffany. "You're his witness?" he asked. Tiffany nodded her head. "Okay, I guess it doesn't get more official then that," he mumbled as he signed and stamped their paperwork. "It will take a few weeks to process, but here's your copy, which will do until you get your certificate in the mail, but I now pronounce you husband and wife. Congratulations Mister and Miss Renado." He said as he extended his hand. David shook his hand firmly. "Thank you sir." As the three left the building, Jennifer reached into her purse and put a veil on her head.

David opened the doors for the girls before getting in his seat. "Master, when we get home, can I put my stuff in your room?" Jennifer asked excitedly. David nodded. "Of course you can," he answered as he started the ignition. As he drove home, Tiffany was smiling as she looked at the ocean, while Jennifer sang along with the music playing on the radio, meanwhile, Elena couldn't help but smile at the behavior of everyone around her. Secretly in her heart, she longed to be so blissfully unconcerned about the world.

As they pulled into the driveway, Summer waited for them, holding Brian as Aidan hung on the clothesline pole by his legs. "How did it go?" she asked. Just then, Jennifer ran around the van, still wearing her veil. Together, the seven of them went into the house. "Elena, are you staying for dinner?" Jennifer asked. Elena shook her head. "I really should get back home, I don't want Ryan to worry," she answered reluctantly. "You've been gone all afternoon, and he hasn't come by once to check on you, so maybe he doesn't care if you check on him," Summer retorted. Elena looked at David. "I think David has enough women to worry about." "Don't be too sure about that," Tiffany interjected. "He can definitely handle himself. Plus, we'd really like you to stay."

Elena tried hard not to cry as she put on a stoic face. "Fuck it, get me a drink," she said, walking into the kitchen. As the four women sat on the couch talking, David took Aidan and Brian outside. "I have to know, how does David keep up with three of you at once?" Elena asked as she took a drink. Tiffany looked to the others before responding. "Well, we all take care of things around the house, so there isn't much for one person to do." "No, I mean how does he have the stamina to handle all three of you?" she clarified. Jennifer smiled as she looked at Tiffany. "I don't think he's the one that struggles to keep up, I mean, I've been bedridden because of him several times." "And I've passed out on him more than once," Summer added. Everyone looked at Tiffany expectantly. "Well, I've never gone that far, but I've had to endure him for several hours on more than one occasion." Elena nearly spit out her drink. "What? How does he do it?" she asked as she leaned close. "Well, he just wouldn't stop, like he has superhuman endurance." Jennifer laughed. "I know how that feels, I thought I was going to die," she laughed.

Summer stared blankly as she thought of something. "Have you ever realized how strong he is?" she asked. Tiffany nodded as Jennifer sat back. "I know he knows how to fight," Jennifer said. "And I've seen him move really quick," Tiffany added. Summer sighed. "David isn't just strong, he's graceful. Like everything he does is effortless, it doesn't seem right." "He's like that in class too. Like he already knows what's coming," Elena added. Tiffany sat quietly, looking at her lap as if deep in thought. "You know, I think I know why that is," she muttered. Elena looked at Tiffany inquisitively. "What are you talking about?" Tiffany stood up quickly, heading to the bookshelf in the dining room. As Tiffany opened the book, Elena looked closely at the pages. "Is that some kind of foreign language?" she asked. "No, shut up and listen." Tiffany turned the pages until she stopped at a specific part. "Here it says, I realized that not only do I know everything I've learned, not only does my body remember everything I've experienced, but my muscles do as well." Jennifer looked at the book, then at Tiffany. "What does that mean?" "I wasn't sure when I first read it, but David said he remembered everything, right? Well, maybe his whole body was like, forced into himself as a child," Tiffany said. "Wouldn't he just grow into it and be like a normal adult once he got older?" Jennifer asked. Summer's eyes got wide suddenly. "Not if he spent the past twelve years building on that foundation."

Elena looked at the other girls, completely lost. "What the fuck are you three talking about? Summer took a deep breath as she grabbed Elena by the shoulder. "If you tell anyone what I'm about to tell you, including David and he finds out, I'm going to hate you forever." "Hate her, David will kill her!" Tiffany exclaimed. "Chill out! I promise I won't say anything, alright," Elena pleaded. Summer took a deep breath. "The reason why he knows everything already is obvious, because he's done this before. He's been married, he's had children, he's already been through this course, he's watched his family die, he even knew who you were before we knew him."

"Are you sure he didn't just say that to take advantage of you?" Elena asked. "No, I'm pretty sure he hated me," Summer said. "I kind of stalked him," Tiffany added. "And I simply refused to leave," Jennifer said. "I think I'm going to need another drink," Elena announced holding up an empty glass. As Tiffany went to get another drink for Elena, David walked in the back door. "Good afternoon ladies, how are y'all doing?" Jennifer jumped up. "Good. Master, can I ask you a question?" "Of course, what do you want to know?" "What do you think about another joining us?" she asked. David didn't even hesitate. "You know my position, they forfeit, or they can fuck off," he responded dismissively as he got himself a drink.

Elena watched curiously as David glided through the kitchen with ease, her view of him now completely tinted by their conversation, though she wasn't sure if she believed it. Leaning toward Summer, she asked. "What's his position?" Summer leaned over and whispered into her ear. "I think it's time to start dinner," Tiffany suddenly announced. Elena got up to help Tiffany as Jennifer went to the bathroom.

As Dinner was being served, Summer brought Aidan and Brian inside. "Where's Jennifer?" Summer asked as she looked around. "Probably masturbating," Tiffany muttered. Elena sat on the opposite side of the table, a clear vantage point to the rest of the house. "Tiffany, I have a question," Elena said, squinting her eyes. "What is it?" "Is Jennifer bisexual?" she asked. Tiffany thought a moment. "Yeah, I think she is. Why?" "I just figured." Just then, David came walking into the dining room. "Good evening ladies. Wow, you did a really good job today," he commented. "Thank you sir. Several minutes later, Jennifer sat next to Elena, an exhausted smile on her face.

After the group ate dinner, Elena told everyone goodnight, taking a wrapped portion home with her. Meanwhile, Jennifer was bathing the boys as David washed the dishes.

Tiffany and Summer were setting up their room, switching Jennifer's clothes with Tiffany's. As it got late, David dressed the boys and put them into bed as Jennifer promptly went to sleep. Summer and Tiffany hadn't actually shared a room before, so the two of them were getting adjusted in their newly arranged space.

Over the next four months, David continued to excel in class, often receiving favorable treatment from the teaching staff and military cadre at his company. Additionally, Sergeant McKeen began to seriously reconsider her plan to intentionally fail the proficiency test, studying during her free time. Brian started walking without help and Aidan was more determined than ever to dig his hole. Meanwhile, Summer had been working at a local pharmacy as a part time pharmacist on the peninsula while Tiffany and Jennifer took care of the children at home.

During the summer between Brian's first birthday and Aidan's third birthday, David had planned to spend the weekend helping Aidan dig his hole, and as usual, Elena would come to visit. Summer was working late at the pharmacy and Jennifer was seven months pregnant, so Tiffany was left to tend to most of the household responsibilities as David played with the boys. "So, he's just going to dig a hole?" Elena asked, staring out the window. "Yep, that's the plan," Tiffany answered. "Hmmm, and you don't think it's weird?" she asked. "No, digging a hole seems like a guy thing to do, but what's weird is that Aidan is the one that suggested it," Tiffany retorted. "How is that weird?" Jennifer asked. Tiffany grabbed the same large book from the shelf and opened it up. "Because right here it says. I decided to dig a hole for fun, the soft dirt made it easy and in just a day, the hole was six feet deep by four feet wide and the boys had a blast playing in it," she read.

Tiffany closed the book. "David never mentioned this before, but he wrote it down. So how would Aidan know to come up with such a suggestion?" she asked rhetorically. Elena watched Jennifer crocheting on the couch as Tiffany made lunch. "Have you guys considered getting a bigger house?" she asked. Without looking up, Jennifer responded. "I like how cozy it is here." Tiffany considered before answering. "David said we can rent a bigger house when we move to Arizona in the winter, but he plans on building an even bigger house when he retires." Where is he building his house?" Elena asked. Tiffany smiled. "Probably close to home," she answered as she placed an assortment of sandwiches on a tray.

"Jennifer, can you tell David that lunch is ready?" Tiffany asked. Elena stood up. "It's okay, I can tell him," she said as she walked out the back door. Elena looked around for David, but couldn't see him. As she examined the hill behind the house, she spotted Aidan and Brian jumping back and forth under the trees. After walking closer, she finally spotted David, digging a massive hole, now more than six feet deep and squared off. "How are the kids supposed to get down there?" she asked. David stopped for a moment before answering. "I'm going to make stairs," he answered, pointing behind him. "Oh, well, Tiffany said it's time for lunch," Elena said as she examined the hole. "Okay, we'll be in shortly," he responded.

As Elena walked into the back door, Jennifer looked up at her. "How's the hole?" she asked. Elena sat down with a profound expression. "How long ago did he start digging that hole?" she asked, looking at Tiffany. "I don't know, right after Summer left a couple hours ago, why?" Elena smiled. "Because he's already dug out, like a six foot cube of dirt," she said. Jennifer stood up to go look at the hole as David and the boys removed their shoes just outside. "Can I see the hole?" Jennifer asked, grabbing onto him. David shook his head. "We had to cover it, so it will have to wait until after lunch," he said as he sat down.

David ate his lunch quickly, occasionally correcting Brian as he tried to disassemble his sandwich. Aidan ate just like his father, even insisting on having the same meats and cheeses, which the girls found adorable. Jennifer ate her lunchmeat rolled in lettuce while the other girls couldn't care less. After everyone ate, David got ready to go back outside as Jennifer put on her shoes. "I want to see the hole," she said excitedly. So, David took Jennifer and the boys outside and lifted the large wooden cover, revealing a massive hole. As Jennifer entered the house, she walked with a sense of accomplishment as if she herself dug the hole. "What are you smiling for?" Elena asked, looking at Jennifer bewildered. Jennifer plopped onto the couch, picking up her yarn and hook. "I have the best husband in the world," she responded audaciously.

Tiffany rolled her eyes as Elena frowned. "But look at you, you're barefoot and pregnant. Is this the life you always wanted?" she asked. Jennifer nodded as if it was all part of her master plan. "I love my life, breeding with my Master is the most fulfilling thing I've ever done. Just look at Summer, she's a big shot pharmacist and I'm sure Tiffany has no complaints," Jennifer said confidently. Elena looked at Tiffany. "What do you do?" she asked. Tiffany thought for a moment before answering. "I like keeping the house in order, and David lets me run things how I see fit." "Well, I think it's really impressive, where did you learn how to do all of this?" Elena asked. Tiffany smiled bashfully. "David taught me."

Elena looked at her in disbelief. "What exactly did he teach you?" Tiffany went to the refrigerator and poured two drinks. "Hey! Can I get something to drink too?" Jennifer pleaded. Tiffany went to the refrigerator and poured three drinks, handing one to Jennifer before sitting down. "When I first met David, he was already mature, something I found very intriguing. He taught my mother and I how to cook and store food, something neither of us were particularly good at. It wasn't until after we got married that it got intense. He has always been organized, and he cleaned everything, so following his lead was natural. There were a few times we butted heads, but he made me promise to obey him without question. So, once I got over myself, everything became so much easier," she said confidently.

Jennifer approached the table and sat down. "Elena, why don't you just get a divorce and stay with us?" she asked sincerely. Elena was dumbstruck at her words. "What! No, I don't think David would allow that, plus how would I even contribute?" "Well, you come over all the time already, so would it be so different? Plus, we could take care of you," Jennifer said. "But wouldn't I belong to David?" she asked. Tiffany held her hand. "I know what you're thinking and he's not like that," Tiffany explained, reassuringly. "Look, if you pass your test, we'll all be going in the same direction either way, you can stay with us during that time, and if you don't like it, then you can leave," she added. Elena considered her words. "Okay, I'll think about it.

Elena left before Tiffany started dinner and David had finished his hole, creating a miniature underground bunker for his children to play in. After dinner was finished, everyone showered and settled in for the night. After dark, Summer arrived and ate leftovers before taking a shower, meanwhile, Jennifer had agreed to switch with Tiffany for the night, allowing Tiffany the opportunity to spend time with David in bed.

Over the next year, Jennifer gave birth to her second son David junior in the early fall. Elena divorced her husband at Jennifer and Tiffany's insistence, and decided to stay with Tiffany and the girls. After completing their advanced training, the entire group moved to Texas. At Summer's request, they were able to find a three thousand square foot six bedroom house with three bathrooms on the south side of the city. However, despite having the extra room, Tiffany and Summer refused to separate.

Chapter 23

The Ire of Competition

After moving into their new house, David's first order of business was to get Elena her own set of furniture and an additional set for their guest bedroom, as well as a bedroom set for Aidan's own room. David's process was methodical, ensuring each bedroom was just like the other. Solid sturdy furniture, a high quality hybrid mattress and an elevated bed frame, alleviating the need for box springs while providing additional storage space. Each room had a work desk and chair, as well as a bookshelf and four-drawer dresser. Initially, Elena was appalled at the sight of her room and furniture getting cleared out, but as she watched it come back together, she began to see the charm of David's motives. Nothing he invested in was generic or uncomfortable, and the more she thought about it, the more she felt like she had fallen into an upscale boarding house.

"Elena, I'm about to go to the store, would you like a lock for your door?" David asked. Elena was taken aback. "Do you think I need it?" she asked. "I can't speak for you, but the girls here have a cracked door policy," he explained. Elena sighed, since she started staying with them, David never bothered her, and she always kept her door shut when she was in her room. "I think I'll be okay," she said. Tiffany ordered pizza for dinner and David left for the store, taking Aidan with him. "What's the cracked door policy?" Elena asked. As Summer unpacked, she turned to Tiffany. "That means if a door is cracked, anybody can just walk in," she explained. "Oh, does that include David?" she asked. Summer thought. "I guess it still applies, but it's more for us girls, and I've never actually shut my door completely since living with them," she said.

After two days, everyone had gotten everything unpacked and the food and household items had been replenished. David and Elena still had two weeks before they were required to sign in to their unit, so David planned another food preparation weekend, something Elena had never participated in before. Before the weekend, David wrote a simple menu and left it on the fridge, requesting ideas and input from others. Of course, each of the girls had their favorites and some even wrote several menu choices. "So, what do I do, just write what I want?" Elena asked, looking at the list. Jennifer nodded. "Yes, whatever you want, and if it can be prepped, he'll add it to the menu." Jennifer answered. Elena thought hard before coming to a decision, writing her food on the list.

After David typed out the shopping list, he summoned Summer and Elena. "You two are coming with me to the store, we have one hour to get everything on the list, if you can't find it, just let me know and we'll go somewhere else," he said as he printed three copies. Together the three got into the van and drove to the store. "David, are we only allowed to get stuff on the list?" Elena asked. "No, but what else do you want to get?" he asked. "I don't know yet," she answered, hesitantly. "I'll tell you what, how about you come with me today, Summer will start in produce and work her way over. You and I will start on the opposite end, and we'll meet in the middle. If you find something you want, just put it in the cart, otherwise, text Summer. Because if you suddenly decide to go galivanting through the store, wasting my time, I'm leaving you here, and it's a long walk," he said coldly. Elena sat back, afraid to respond. "Hey, there are always better times for that kind of shopping, plus it gives us an excuse to have girl time," Summer said, reassuring her.

As they got to the store, Elena looked over the list, everything was grouped by food type and written like a restaurant inventory sheet. Before they even entered the store, she could tell this was going to be a learning experience. David gestured for Summer to grab three carts, handing one to Elena and taking one for himself. Before setting off, he grabbed Summer by the throat. "Make me proud Summer," he said as he kissed her. "Yes sir," she purred as she pressed her forehead into his. As David set off, Elena struggled to keep up, watching him as he quickly filled each cart with robotic efficiency. By the time they reached the sauces and condiments, David ran into Summer. "Did you get every-thing?" he asked. Looking at the list, Summer sighed. "No sir, they didn't have any bean sprouts," she answered. Summer looked at Elena. "Did you find something you wanted?" she asked. Elena fumbled as she looked around. "I tried, but we never stopped long enough to think, so I grabbed these creamsicles on impulse," she answered.

David moved to the checkout and began loading everything on the conveyer belt as Summer ran around to the other side with an empty cart, putting the filled bags into the cart. After checking out, the three of them pushed the three carts to the van and began loading the groceries. David looked to Elena. "Go ahead and start the van," he commanded, handing her the keys. Summer pushed the first two carts to the cart return before returning to the van and climbing in the passenger seat. "Is he always like this when he goes shopping?" Elena asked. "No, only when we food prep," Summer answered. Elena let out a deep breath. "Thank god!" she sighed. "I'm kidding, he's like this every time he goes shopping," Summer said as she chuckled.

Once they got home, everyone with the exception of Brian and little David came running out to carry in the groceries. Elena marveled at their efficiency as she watched everyone unload bags, several at a time. Within an hour, everyone was already doing their part. Tiffany and Summer were cutting vegetables, while Jennifer prepared the pasta and soup. Meanwhile, David was cutting and trimming meat with frightful precision as Elena watched, marveling at the cacophony of culinary wizards. "Elena, I need you to start cooking rice, just use the rice cooker in the cabinet." He ordered. "What do I do with the rice once it's done?" she asked as she took out the rice cooker. "When you're finished, spread it on a sheet pan and put it in the refrigerator, but don't press it, it needs to be loose. Then make another batch, I need at least three batches," he said.

Elena never actually considered the amount of work they put into cooking before, as food was always prepared by one of the others, and she had never helped with the food prep when they lived in Arizona, because she was typically visiting her family when they did. By Sunday afternoon, they had completely filled the freezer with meals and the rest of the food was sorted and organized in the refrigerator and cabinets.

That next week, Aidan would have his fourth birthday and wanted to go to the lake for a picnic, much to the delight of everyone else. Tiffany was especially excited as she had not had the chance to go swimming in several years, however, she would prefer to go to the waterpark, but after explaining the waterparks policy on small children, she decided against it this time. As the girls went swimsuit shopping, David was home, testing his children in the above ground pool he purchased for Aidan two years prior. Despite Aidan's age, he showed an unnatural proficiency in many advanced motor skills, to include swimming, as if he already knew how. Brian and little David were the same, limited only by their size and physical disposition. David suspected that he somehow passed on his retrospective knowledge and experience, but never found evidence that they possessed any individual memories from his past life or his children's past life, other than the occasional dream or emotional bond. For this reason, David would constantly challenge and test his children's strength, abilities and understanding. Additionally, this is also why he strongly considered homeschooling his children, at least until their teenage years.

Meanwhile, at the department store, Tiffany, Jennifer, Summer and Elena were shopping for swimsuits. In order to satisfy David's need for structure and familiarity, none of the three girls even considered looking at swimsuits outside of their respective color pallet. Something they knew made him very comfortable. Elena, on the other hand, couldn't understand why they wouldn't diverge. Following the un-spoken rule of women in groups, Elena was subconsciously strong-armed into finding a swimsuit that wasn't red, blue, or white colored, ultimately settling on a very dark green bikini. Summer settled on an Ark one-piece with a cross back in white, and Tiffany got a low waisted red halter top bikini, while Jennifer picked a mid-waisted royal blue one-piece with an open back.

As the girls left the department store, Tiffany touched the cameo on her neck. "We need to make another stop," she said suddenly. "What is it?" Jennifer asked concerned. "I need to get a choker for swimming," she said, pointing at the choker on her neck. Summer's eyes widened. "I should probably get one too," she added. Jennifer smiled as she reached up and grabbed the eternity collar around her neck. Standing off to the side, Elena chuckled. "You ladies are something else," she said. With shopping bags in their hands, the four women walked into the mall's concourse, like a group of divas on a nighttime drama.

Back at home, Aidan had more than proven his skill in swimming, not just in his technique, but endurance as well. Brian, however, lacked the lung capacity to sustain long term underwater swimming, but his baby fat made him buoyant enough to be able to tread water much easier than Aidan. Little David was almost completely buoyant in the water, but because of his underdeveloped limbs and joints, could only move short distances in the water and his small lung capacity limited his underwater swimming to only a few seconds. Despite this, all three boys handled the water with familiarity, never once panicking or sinking. Even with their swimming aptitude, there was no guarantee they would be able to swim against the water current and the opaque water would certainly make it difficult for them to see where they're going.

The ladies had just finished their shopping when they decided to stop by the food court for a snack when Tiffany's phone rang. "Hello. Yes sir. Okay. They did? I can do that, sure.

I'll see you when we get home." Tiffany hung up the phone. "Was that Master? Does he need something?" Jennifer asked. "He wanted us to pick up two swimming trainers for the younger boys," Tiffany responded. "What about Aidan?" Summer asked. "It honestly wouldn't surprise me if he could breathe under water," Tiffany answered. After stopping by the store to pick up swim trainers, The girls went home, catching David in the kitchen as he got drinks for the boys, now freshly showered.

"Did you ladies have a fun time shopping today?" he asked. One by one, all of his girls greeted him, kissing him as they responded. Elena, still standing there, watched as the three women greeted him uniquely and affectionately, unshaken by the rivalry of the others. After putting their bags in their rooms, everyone returned to the living room. As they sat on the couch, Aidan, Brian and little David enthusiastically shared details about their day, indiscriminate to their audience. "Aunt Summer, Daddy said I can swim with him," Aidan said proudly, as he twirled his finger in her hair. "Oh, you think you can keep up with Daddy?" she asked. Aidan nodded proudly.

"I'm going to make dinner tonight, so you all can relax," David announced, as he walked into the kitchen. Aidan and Brian turned on the TV, and started playing video games, while Tiffany and the rest went upstairs to show off their swimsuits. As David was cutting and tenderizing the chicken, Elena walked to the refrigerator to get a drink. "What are you making for dinner?" she asked. "Chicken parmesan," he answered. Elena smiled. "I've always liked chicken parmesan, but I never knew how it was made," she said, taking a drink. David stopped. "Well, I can teach you, if you'd like," he said smiling. She considered for a moment.

"Fuck it. I'm here, might as well," she stated as she set her drink down.

The morning of Aidan's birthday, David was packing the van as the girls shuffled around, trying to wake up. David had already made breakfast, which made Elena feel guilty. However, the others simply sat at the table, seemingly unphased by the spread laid out before them. Elena watched as Tiffany plated food for the boys as Jennifer picked at the plate full of bacon, next to Summer hovering over a plate of waffles, covered in fruit. "Why do you three seem so out of it this morning?" Elena asked, observing the other three. "Ask Tiffany," Summer mumbled. Looking at Tiffany, she asked again. "What happened last night?" she asked, looking at Tiffany, who smiled mischievously.

After several minutes of explanation, Elena sat back in her chair. "So, he actually did that?" she asked, blushing. Tiffany nodded her head. "I couldn't stop cumming, it was actually kind of terrifying," she said as she smiled, taking a sip of her coffee. "We should really congratulate Summer," Jennifer said, holding up her glass. "Shut up Jennifer, that doesn't count, you lesbian whore," Summer barked. "What did Summer do?" Elena asked, leaning forward. Jennifer smiled after looking at Summer, who rolled her eyes. "So, Master told Summer to hold me down so he could fuck me, but then Summer kept cumming on me the whole time, I mean, I could feel her splashing me over and over again." Summer huffed. "It wasn't my fault, he held me down and put that stupid toy in me, I couldn't help it," Summer said defensively. "Is that why you kept fainting?" Jennifer asked. Summer just rolled her eyes. "I thought you were doing it yourself. Hmm, that's probably why Master slapped your ass every time you fainted," Jennifer chuckled.

Elena sat in silence, squirming in her seat. "I need to use the bathroom," she announced. As she left, Tiffany and Jennifer smiled. "All right ladies, the van is packed," he announced, walking into the living room. "Thank you for making breakfast," Jennifer said as she hugged him. Patting her head, he looked around. "Where's Elena?" he asked. "She just went to the bathroom," Summer answered. "Probably masturbating," Tiffany added. After everyone was ready, they all began to get into the van.

After arriving at their picnic location, David parked the van, set up the barbeque pit, and erected the awning over the table. During this time, everyone put on sunblock while Tiffany and Jennifer put sunblock on the boys. David wanted to go to the beach first, so he didn't set up the picnic area completely and they all headed toward the designated swimming area, carrying bags as David carried half a dozen folding chairs. Upon their arrival, he setup a spot close to the water and unfolded the chairs before removing his shirt and shoes to join the boys, eliciting a series of whistles and objectifying comments from his women.

Brian and little David had to get use to the trainers, but eventually learned to handle the buoyancy as they swam and splashed in the water. Aidan, on the other hand, immediately swam all the way to the edge of the swimming area, playing on the buoy. As David entered the water, he immediately began throwing Brian and little David in different directions, each time swimming back to him. Tiffany, having taken a page out of the book of David, pulled four sun hats from her carry bag, handing them out to her sisters and Elena. "Thank you Madam Tiffany," Jennifer responded. One by one, all four women began removing their outer garments, leaving nothing but their swimsuits, chokers, hats and sunglasses. "Are you going to swim?" Elena asked, unfamiliar with this area. "No, not yet, the water's still too cold," Tiffany responded.

After more than an hour, David and the boys returned to the beach and began drying off when he realized just how unbelievable the sight was. All four women, sitting side by side, looked like sisters. As David picked up a drink out of his bag, he pointed. "You four look like sorority sisters," he commented. "How do we look like sorority sisters?" Summer asked, tilting her head. David looked closer. "I think it's the matching hats," looking down the line, he just realized that each one had corresponding chokers, other than Jennifer, but to his surprise, even Elena wore a choker. David smiled before asking, "Is everybody ready for lunch?" he asked. Everybody nodded. "Okay, I'm going to get things going, should take me about an hour, so y'all can stay here while I get that done if you want," he said before departing.

As David was preparing lunch, the crowd started to grow, especially around the beach, while campers began to occupy the surrounding picnic tables, which caused David to reminisce. Meanwhile, on the beach, Jennifer and Tiffany joined the boys in the water as Summer and Elena remained seated. Without fail, Summer and Elena drew the attention of a large group of onlookers. "Hey, we were about to start a game of volleyball, but we don't have enough players, would you two be interested in joining?" one of them asked. Summer declined, but after persisting for several minutes, Tiffany responded, standing behind them. "We'll play," she said. Both men turned in the direction of the voice, and as if cursed by the boner gods, began to stammer. "Oh, okay. Uh, awesome." they answered. "Give us fifteen minutes and we'll meet you at the volleyball net," she demanded.

As David was preparing the food, Jennifer approached with all three children in tow. "Hey, how are y'all doing?" he asked. Jennifer smiled. "Tiffany just drafted us for a volleyball game," she said. "Do you want my help?" he asked. Jennifer shook her head, "No, I think we got this, besides, I don't think they're interested in volleyball," she said, hinting at their intentions. David thought a moment, "Alright, I'll be there in half an hour," he said. Before leaving, Jennifer kissed him, leaving the boys at the table. "You guys want to help daddy cook?" he asked.

At the volleyball net, a crowd suddenly began to form as four hot women in swimsuits faced off against four young men. A spectacle most people would pay to see. "Tiffany, why did you agree to play?" Summer asked. Tiffany looked at Summer, "Because in this state, volleyball is a fundamental sport in all girl's athletics, plus, I don't think they really know how to play," she said. Jennifer smiled, as she hadn't considered this, but agreed. "Even if we don't win, it could still be fun," she said. As they got ready to play, Tiffany called the terms, "One set!" As the game began, David could hear the cheering from his table as he prepared the food.

Just as promised, David showed up after thirty minutes, sitting on the side with his boys. The score was 21 to 18 in favor of the girls. David was pleased to see his team winning, but was more pleased at the sight of his women sweating in their swimsuits, rolling in the sand. Surprisingly, Jennifer had quite the arm for serving, while Tiffany, Summer and Elena's height gave them a notable advantage in jumping. Relying on their upper body strength, the other team often overserved or lost control of the ball due to lack of practice. In less than ten minutes, the game was over. As the game ended, Brian and little David rushed to their mother while Aidan stayed by David's side. As David approached, Jennifer jumped into David's arms, kissing him as he held her.

Meanwhile, the other team noticed and approached. "Your wife has quite the arm on her," one said, as the others began looking toward the other three women. As David engaged in small talk, he realized that their group had already divvied up the girls and were preparing to shoot their shot. Jennifer, still clinging to David, began sucking on his ear. "Master, I want you to break me again," she whispered. David set her down. "Later, right now, take Brian and David to get the chairs and meet me back at the table, lunch is waiting," he ordered. "Yes Master!" she responded. As she turned to leave, he approached Tiffany with Aidan, still talking with her designated suitor.

Completely disregarding their conversation, he grabbed Tiffany by the throat, pulling her close as he kissed her. "Lunch is ready," he said. Tiffany blushed. "Yes sir," she responded as she took Aidan back. Turning toward the other two, he smiled. Summer and Elena, desperate to escape their situation, had noticed his actions up to this point. "Summer, Elena!" he called out. Both girls approached, side by side. "Lunch is ready, join the rest so we can eat," he commanded. Summer grabbed him as she kissed him. "Yes sir," she said, smiling as she dragged her fingers down his chest. To David's surprise, even Elena reached out to kiss him, holding the back of his head, as she leaned toward his ear. "Thank you," she whispered.

The other group watched in ire as four women threw themselves at David, one after the other. Arriving back at the table, everybody ate their lunch, then spent the rest of the afternoon swimming and playing on the beach. As the sun began to go down, David and the girls packed everything and headed home.

Chapter 24

The Burden of Trust

It's been a month since David had arrived at his organization and because he was too late to join his unit during their deployment process, he and Elena were assigned to the rear detachment. Jennifer decided that since she had not had the chance to visit her mother since getting married, she would go for a visit on the week of David junior's birthday, taking Brian with her. Tiffany insisted on tagging along, eager to visit her mother with Aidan as well. Meanwhile, Summer had just become pregnant and even though she had no intention of taking time off of work yet, wanted to visit her father before she began to show, this left David home alone with Elena, something David felt was suspiciously convenient.

With only two of them in the house, Elena began to miss the company of the others. As the two sat on the couch, eating their dinner, Elena kept glancing at David, who seemed completely unaffected by the quiet. "Is it hard for you to be alone, now that everybody is gone?" she asked. David shook his head. "No, I'm actually more use to it than you might realize," he responded. David paused for a moment. "However, being in such a big empty house does feel a bit unnerving," he said, looking around. Elena took a deep breath. "They told me that you've done this before," she muttered. "I figured," he said without looking up. "Am I in trouble?" she asked, a concerned look on her face. David shook his head. "No, we actually got along before," he answered, surprising her. "We did?" she responded with a shocked look on her face. David nodded. "Do you know what happened to me?" she asked. "I heard from one of our classmates that even though you intentionally failed the test you still deployed and divorced your husband," he responded. After they finished their dinner, he washed their dishes and took a shower, then went to his room.

Elena was in her room, unable to sleep, so she picked up her phone and sent a text message to the other girls. "It's quiet here, I miss you guys." After only a few minutes, she got a response. "We miss you too," Tiffany replied. "It's quiet here too, now go to sleep," Summer replied. After putting down her phone, Elena got up to go to the bathroom. As she stepped out into the hallway, she noticed that all the bedroom doors in the hallway were completely closed, except hers and the master bedroom. After washing her hands, she stepped back into the dark hallway, listening to the silence, which seemed to scream in her head. Closing her eyes for a moment, she took a deep breath and walked toward the door. Entering the room, she shut the door tightly behind her and crawled into bed, pulling the covers over her. David's arm reached around, pulling her close, causing her to gasp slightly. "Goodnight Elena," he whispered. "Goodnight," she responded, falling asleep.

The next morning, Elena woke up and went downstairs to find David heating up a couple of breakfast burritos. "Coffee's done," he said as he packed his bag for work. "Good morning," she replied. Neither one of them mentioned last night, and David's behavior toward her had not changed, making her feel more relieved than frustrated. As he ate his breakfast, Elena made a cup of coffee. "Have you heard from anyone?" she asked. David nodded his head. "Jennifer's mother is disappointed she couldn't make it to the wedding, but Jennifer promised we'd send pictures," he answered. "What are you going to do?" David thought for a moment, "I guess we could rent some formal wear and have a photo shoot. Do you feel like getting dressed up?" he asked. Elena chuckled, shaking her head.

Later that afternoon, David waited for Elena after work as he smoked in the parking lot. After a while, Elena walked out of the back of the building, arms drooping like someone spoiled her favorite show. "What's the matter with you?" he asked. Slumped in her seat, she sighed. "They want to deploy me early, apparently one of the team sergeants got hurt and they need a replacement," she scowled. David remembered this happening to him, but he was able to sidestep it. "I wouldn't worry about that," he said, starting the car. Elena was already crying. "But I didn't want to deploy again, I know you said it happened anyway, but I didn't think it would happen so soon," she said. David grabbed her hand. "I told you not to worry about it. Sergeant Ashburn is going to talk to you tomorrow," he said, trying to reassure her. Elena wiped her eyes and nodded.

After the two got home, David called his girls, and talked to his children before preparing dinner. After Elena got changed, she continued to wallow on the couch, not wanting to eat. "You have to eat something, otherwise you're just going to get hungry later and end up sleeping with food in your stomach," he said. Elena didn't respond and ended up going to bed earlier than normal. Later that night after taking a shower, David went to his room, but as he turned on his light, he saw a body sized bump on the far side of the bed. Apparently, she wasn't going to sleep in her bed tonight either. After getting into bed, he could still hear her sniffling. "I know you were just trying to make me feel better, but what if you're wrong?" she asked. David rolled onto his right side, facing the door. "I'm not wrong," he answered.

The next afternoon as David prepared to leave, Elena was already waiting by the car as he arrived. After unlocking the door and getting in, Elena grabbed his head and kissed him on the cheek. "What was that for?" he asked, feigning surprise. "Sergeant Ashburn said he wanted the deployment slot they gave me," she said excitedly. "Okay, and?" he responded. "You knew this was going to happen," she said, hitting him on the shoulder. David smiled and started the car.

After arriving home, Elena immediately started heating up her meal as she went to change clothes. David was just glad she wasn't moping anymore. As the two ate dinner, Elena was suddenly in the mood to talk. "Did your wife and I get along?" she asked, taking a bite of her food. "No, my ex was very untrusting from the start." "Oh, so she was the jealous type?" David shook his head. "No, she was the untrusting type. Believe it or not, I actually don't mind possessiveness or jealousy. Jennifer's possessive and Tiffany gets Jealous, but they still trust me" he answered. Elena looked at him confused. "I wouldn't think Tiffany was the jealous type. David laughed. "Oh, she is." Elena smiled as she continued eating her food. "I like your little family, your wives are the best and even though I don't like kids, yours are alright. "Gee, thanks," he said sarcastically. "Plus, you do a really good job keeping everything together," she said sincerely. "You're welcome," he said, as he cracked a smile.

Later that night, David was in his bed as he heard his door open. "David, can I sleep with you tonight?" she asked. David wasn't sure why she was suddenly asking, as she hadn't asked the past two nights. "Of course," he answered. After Elena crawled into his bed, she immediately clung to his back, pulling her body into his. As they both laid there, her legs began gliding along his, as if she were trying to either ease him awake or lull him to sleep. When he turned around to face her, she moved her face closer, little by little until he could feel her breath. Elena pushed her leg gently between his knees, until he eventually allowed her to rest her leg between his thighs, still inching closer until he could feel her chest against his. David could feel her body getting hotter as her hands began to move around his.

As she pulled his hand onto her hips, he pressed his face gently against hers, until their lips touched, but did not kiss her. David could feel her heart beating through her shirt as he began to move his hands, cupping her breasts. As if by mistake, she stuck out her tongue so subtly that it gently pressed against his lips, releasing a whirlwind of pent up desire within her. As she felt his mouth open slightly, she gripped him fiercely, pushing her tongue into his mouth. Elena inhaled deeply as she kissed him, lifting her body high as she gripped the sides of his face, until her lungs were full. As she let out her breath, she pressed her tongue against his, and sucked on his lower lip.

David lifted her body effortlessly on top of his own, sitting her up on his stomach. With hasty determination, she removed her shirt and then his, casting them to the ground.

Elena's body was thin, and her breasts were a strong B-cup, her olive skin reflecting the ambient light from the window. After she rolled onto her back to remove her shorts, she immediately turned to remove his. Now completely naked, she climbed into his lap, sitting on his abdomen as she leaned over to kiss him. Slowly at first she grinded her hips back and forth as her vulva glided against the base of his cock, letting out little whimpers as she moved. Gradually speeding up, she held onto his shoulders as her moans got louder and quicker, inching just a tiny bit closer with each thrust of her hips.

As she got closer to climax, her vulva glided off the tip of his cock putting more direct pressure on her clit as she rolled her hips repeatedly. Biting her lip, her whimpers became moans as she suddenly began to tremble, gushing all over him. Noticing this, David reached out and grabbed her neck, rocking her body forward as he kissed her while positioning his cock to penetrate her as she sat back. After letting her go, she sat up, looking slightly behind her as she lowered her body down onto him, completely bottoming out before her ass reached his hips. This initial push made her muscles tighten, as the pain of her vagina stretching over his girth nearly tore through her like a kick to the groin. After the pain subsided, she began to move her body slowly at first, then faster, then harder.

Elena continued to ride him until she came again, this time falling off to his side. As she lied there panting, David moved over top of her, watching her as she slowly caught her breath. However, just as she tried to speak, he lifted her thighs like a quartered watermelon and began devouring her. The faint metallic scent permeated his nose as he licked and sucked out every bit of her own cum he could reach from her deepest parts. Once satisfied, he began fucking her, alternating between long-slow strokes, and vigorous-deep thrusts until he finally found her most animated response. He stayed with this rhythm, until she was so wet, he could hardly feel her.

Then David turned her onto her side, with one leg resting on his shoulder and the other between his legs, using the front of her neck and the back of her hair as leverage, he thrust himself into her aggressively. Still whimpering, and unable to speak, he flipped her onto her knees, pulling her arms behind her as he fucked her from behind. After he filled her up, he watched as her body drained down the inside of her legs until she eventually collapsed.

The next morning, neither David nor Elena talked about what they had done, nor did the way they treat or speak to each other change. However, every night for the rest of the week, David and Elena fucked like college students until after midnight, each day going to bed earlier than the day before. Saturday morning, they picked up where they left off the night before, and continued until almost noon, when David insisted they get some lunch. As he prepared lunch, Elena stripped the bed and started laundry, remaking the bed with clean bedding before coming back downstairs.

As they were eating lunch, Summer walked in the door. "I'm home," she announced, kissing David before she sat next to Elena at the table. "I'm so glad you made lunch, I'm starving," Summer said, taking David's food. "When do you plan on taking maternity leave?" Elena asked. "Probably when I hit my third trimester," Summer answered. Elena smiled as she watched

David making himself another lunch. "How was your visit?" David asked. Still chewing her food, Summer responded, "Boring but necessary."

After several hours, Tiffany and Jennifer arrived, bringing all of the excess noise with them. "Master, I missed you!" Jennifer shouted, jumping into his arms. David kissed Jennifer and set her down before taking a hold of Tiffany and kissing her flamboyantly on the lips. Tiffany laughed as the boys tried to pull her off of him. One by one, he greeted his children and announced their plans for a wedding photo shoot. "We're going to have wedding pictures?" Jennifer asked excitedly. "Yes, I figure we can rent wedding dresses and gowns for each of you, so that way, all we have to do is shuffle people around in different clothes like a fashion show," David explained. Jennifer laughed at the idea, while Summer and Tiffany admired his critical thinking. "Can I have wedding pictures made too?" Summer asked. "Of course you can. Plus, I think it's a good idea to get it done sooner rather than later," David said, gesturing to her belly.

"I just had the greatest idea!" Jennifer said excitedly. "How about we have a picture of all four of us in our wedding dresses next to David." Summer squinched her eyebrows. "Like our prom picture?" she asked. "Yes! Like our prom pictures," Jennifer responded. "We could do that," David said. "Maybe, if she wants, Elena can wear a wedding dress too?" Jennifer added. "Why would she want to wear a wedding dress?" Summer asked. "Cause it could be fun," Jennifer answered. "I think that's up to Elena, so don't go pressuring her," Tiffany said. "Yes Madam Tiffany," she responded. "Hey Elena?" Jennifer said. "Yes Jennifer?" "Have you and Master fucked each other yet?" she asked. Summer gasped at the audacity as Elena blushed. "Jennifer! Don't embarrass her like that!" Tiffany scolded.

Elena's eyes fell, "Why would you ask me something like that?" she asked quietly. "Because I could smell it on you when I got home," Jennifer said shamelessly. David nodded his head, "Yeah, we did a little bit." Elena blushed as the rest of the girls swarmed her, congratulating her and pressing her for details. "Give her some space, she's had a long week," David ordered. "You gave it to her all week?" Jennifer asked before smiling mischievously at Elena. Blushing from ear to ear, she ran to her room, followed by Tiffany.

Tiffany knocked on the door. "Who is it?" "It's me, Tiffany." Elena open the door, then sat back down. "I'm sorry about Jennifer," Tiffany said as she sat down. "I'm not mad at her, I just wasn't prepared to face this so soon," Elena sighed. "I don't think any of us were, but can I ask you a question?" "Sure, go ahead," Elena responded, still uncertain. "Why did you do it?" Tiffany asked. "I don't know, I guess it's been building over the past year or so, and I see how happy you all are, plus something happened that really kind of settled it for me," Elena explained. Tiffany nodded her head. "Yeah, we've all been there, when we first had that experience, I wanted to kiss his feet." Elena laughed. "Ewe, that's gross." "Probably, but I had already given myself to him at that point, but he was gone for a month, so I couldn't."

Elena sat quietly for a moment. "Tiffany, what's your purpose with David? I mean, there's got to be a bigger reason than just being able to know the future," she asked. Tiffany shook her head. "David doesn't actually know the future, he just remembers doing this already. It's not like he can tell what's going to happen, because obviously, being with him is proof the future can be changed." Elena thought a moment. "How far out can he remember?" she asked. "His last memory was when he was 53, so, about 27 more years," she answered. Elena considered as she said, "Obviously he doesn't have the keys to success, because he wouldn't be repeating the same things if he did. So, does he have like, some kind of trick to surviving some kind of disaster we can't escape from?" Tiffany didn't answer. "Oh my god! That's it, isn't it?" Tiffany nodded her head. "Wait, why doesn't he try to stop it?" Tiffany shook her head, "We can't avoid this, none of us can. "So, all we can do is prepare?"

Tiffany grabbed her hands firmly before explaining. "Look, we don't know if he was sent back, or if we just can't remember repeating our life the way he can. So, there might be others out there going through the same thing, but with different intentions. We also don't know why he can remember in the first place. What we do know is that even though he's been through hell, this is the person he is. He's not a tyrant, he takes care of us and he's kind. Just don't get in his way, don't slow him down, and don't question him. If there are others, and they find out what we know, or what we're doing, all of our lives could be at risk, and I'm certain, David will kill as many people as it takes to soothe his wrath, if that's taken from him again." Still trying to process what she heard, Elena asked. "What about our families, can we help them?" Tiffany shook her head. "If we do, then where does it end? The more people we take on, the greater risk there is. Plus, how do you know you can trust them? Can you bear that kind of burden?

Elena sighed deeply before standing up. "We better get back downstairs before everyone else starts to worry." Together the two went back downstairs. As they walked into the living room, Jennifer jumped up. "I'm sorry Elena, I didn't mean to embarrass you," she said, hanging her head. Elena comforted her. "It's okay Jennifer, I just needed a moment, but I'm good now," she said. After hugging Jennifer, Elena walked into the kitchen, where David was cooking dinner. "Are you okay now?" he asked. She approached him and hugged him tightly. "Yes sir, I'm much better."

Two weeks later, David organized a photoshoot with the girls and Elena, each one wearing their own rented wedding dress, while David only had to change his clothes once, as Summer preferred him in his military dress uniform. Each woman was allowed to pick their theme, colors, background and flowers, which made every photo set unique, other than their hair and makeup. Elena alternated between posing as a bridesmaid or maid of honor within the pictures, each time wearing a different dress. In the group picture, which included the boys standing in front, Elena stood to David's left, as the rest stood to his right, from tallest to shortest.

Summer gave birth to a baby girl a month after David's 27th birthday, unfortunately, only one month after returning from paternity leave, he was given deployment orders because one of their team leaders had to be medically evacuated, and David was selected as the replacement. Once David left, Summer went back to work after only eleven weeks of maternity leave, leaving her daughter Lily under the care of her aunts.

Chapter 25

The Mah and Binik Scale

In the fall, David's entire organization was redeploying, and David would be coming home. Aidan was old enough to be in kindergarten, but at David's insistence, was homeschooled by Tiffany and Jennifer. Inevitably, Brian and little David joined, despite them only being two and three years old. Upon David's arrival, his reception was attended by nearly every member of his family, the largest group of people for a single person there, even though he was only deployed for four months. Elena, on the other hand, did not attend, as the rear detachment was in charge of setting up and organizing the redeployment process.

As the battalion entered the gymnasium, organized by company, families watched and cheered as they saw their sons, daughters, or spouses, however, David's group only talked quietly to themselves. Outside the gym, trucks carrying the bags from the airplane were unloaded and organized by company and lined up alphabetically. Elena, who was in charge of this detail, spotted David's bags and quickly put them in her car as her detail continued to work.

After the redeployment ceremony was over, Soldiers rushed to greet their families as David casually walked to his group. Summer cried as she approached, rushing to meet him first, jumping into his arms as Jennifer held Lily. David held her for a moment as she kissed him all over his head and face. After setting her down, he took Lily from Jennifer, kissed her on the forehead and promptly handed Lily to Summer, picking up Jennifer in his arms. "David, Elena said she has your bags," Tiffany said, looking at her phone. David nodded, setting Jennifer back down. After kissing Tiffany, the group left, as several witnesses who had seen his greeting, watched him leave, a look of disbelief on their faces.

On the way home, Summer drove the van and David sat in the passenger seat. "Did you have fun while you were gone?" she asked. "It was just as I remembered with a few small exceptions, however, I did enjoy the warm weather," he said. "When do you have to go back?" Jennifer asked. "We deploy again next fall, after the brigade reorganizes, so, about a year," he answered. "Do you think Elena will deploy too?" Summer asked. "Most likely, but I don't know where she's going to be assigned, so we'll have to see," he responded.

After they got home, Tiffany unbuckled Lily from her seat and handed her to Summer, then together they all went inside. Summer had moved into Elena's room with Lily and Elena moved in with Tiffany, converting the spare room into a homeschool room. However, as David changed out of his uniform, he noticed some of his own clothes were missing from his closet and drawers. Dismissing the thought for now, he quickly changed and went downstairs. "How are the boys doing with school?" he asked. Tiffany lowered her head as she approached him. "I haven't found their milestone yet, so we're just testing for now," she answered, running her hands over his shoulders.

Before David deployed, his instructions were simple, assess their aptitude for learning first, then teach them the five major subjects: Mathematics, English, Reading, Sciences, and History. All three boys already knew their alphabet, colors, shapes, how to count, and even how to write, so he assumed their skills in these areas would naturally improve with practice, however, he did not expect them to know these subjects, because he believed that education influenced memory rather than experience. As it turns out, counting is not a memory, but a skill, just as mathematics is simply an advanced counting skill. Understanding this dilemma, David decided to produce another plan and discuss it at a later date.

For now, David realized that he had more pressing matters to take care of, he had been gone for four months, and everyone needed quality time. Jennifer made lunch and as they all sat down to eat, David opened the conversation. "I have tomorrow off, but the next two days, we have our redeployment processing, once that's finished, everyone will get two weeks of block leave, then I have to go back to work." Nobody responded, and everyone watched him, wide eyed and expectantly for him to continue. "Does anyone here have something they need to get done?" he asked. "I have to work, but I took this week off," Summer said. "When do you start?" he asked. "Today," she answered. Tiffany raised her hand. "Elena was able to take next week off," she said. David thought for a moment. "Summer, when do you go back to work?" he asked. "Wednesday," she replied. "Okay, we have four days where all of us are going to be off together, so we can plan something then, after that, we're on our own," he said in a serious tone.

"Master, is there anything we can do until then?" Jennifer asked. "I'm glad you brought that up, I have a few things I'd like to get done, but we'll have a meeting at dinner to discuss them, but after we get done eating here, I want you to start checking ads, and find me two Dachshund puppies, female preferably," he said. Jennifer started bouncing with excitement as Summer asked. "Puppies? You want two wiener dogs?" David nodded his head. After finishing his lunch, he stood up. "Summer, meet me in my room in ten minutes," he said as he walked away. Summer looked at Tiffany, then at Jennifer. "I wonder what he wants to talk about?" Summer asked.

An hour and a half later, Summer walked back into the living room. Jennifer was on the computer searching ads and listings as Summer threw herself onto the couch. Tiffany, who was playing a game with the boys looked up. "How did it go?" she asked. "You'll see, he wants you to go see him next," Summer said. As Tiffany went upstairs, Jennifer was writing contact information on a sheet of paper and sent several messages to several pet owners and breeders. Meanwhile, Summer walked over to take over Tiffany's spot on her game with the boys. After nearly two hours, Tiffany came downstairs and noticed the boys had gone from their board game to the television, watching animal planet. Jennifer was back on the couch crocheting winter clothes for Lily when Tiffany sat next to her. "You're next Jennifer," Tiffany said, seemingly out of breath. Jennifer tried to contain her excitement as she nearly tripped, trying to run up the stairs.

Elena arrived as Jennifer came down, grinning from ear to ear. "I'm home," Elena said as she dropped the bags near the door. "Good, David wants you to go see him, so you might as well just head up," Jennifer said. Elena left the bags, and with a concerned look on her face, ran upstairs.

As Elena was upstairs, Summer started dinner, and Tiffany went back to playing with the boys as Jennifer got back to her project. Elena stopped at her room to remove her boots, but as she entered David's room, the first thing she noticed was his complete state of undress, making the bed. "David, you wanted to, Whoa! Umm, you wanted to see me?" she asked, suddenly blushing." "Take off your uniform," he commanded. Elena didn't waste time and immediately stripped down to her underwear. Standing sheepishly in front of his door, he gestured to the bed. "Get down on your knees and put your hands in your lap," he continued. Again, Elena obeyed without saying a word.

As Elena waited on the floor, he picked up a long black scarf wrapping it around her eyes, blindfolding her. As she sat in darkness, every sound felt sharp, causing her to jump as he carelessly opened drawers and dropped things in front of her. She wanted to reach her hand out, but was afraid to move her body as David continued to move around her in silence. Suddenly, she felt a tug against the bun on the back of her head as his cock immediately filled her mouth. The sudden inability to breathe felt like pressure building in her lungs as she quickly adjusted her throat to take him in. Ruthlessly, he slid his cock down her throat, pushing and pulling her head as she clenched her fists.

Once satisfied, he lifted her body into the air from behind. As she lowered her legs, he removed her underwear and bent her over the foot of the bed. "Don't move," he commanded. Do I respond? She thought as she felt bands wrap around her wrists and ankles, the sound of metal buckles clinking together. "Relax your shoulders," he said calmly as he rotated her arms out to the side, the smell of the women before her soaked into the bedding under her face.

With a zipping sound, both of her arms, followed by both of her feet, were pulled tight against the corners, pulling her body tight against the foot of the bed, over the footboard. Fear and uncertainty began to fill her thoughts as her breathing deepened. Whap! With a sharp crack, her body felt a stinging on her lower back as if he slapped her with a handful of tiny whips. Just then, a rigid but soft object easily slid inside of her, it didn't feel like his cock, but before she could guess, the buzzing toy began to vibrate up her pelvis and down her legs.

Whap! The same stinging, this time on her thigh. As the vibrator's intensity increased, pushed against her clitoris, she struggled to separate the feeling of pleasure and pain. Whap! Before she realized it was happening, she came, the sensation making her tender skin tingle as he continued to hit her. David whipped her repeatedly with his flogger, covering her entire body with red marks. Elena stopped wincing from the pain as her skin started to feel hot and numb while she continued to cum intermittently.

Elena reflexively pulled her body tight as her orgasm seemed to flow throughout her skin, releasing through every point of impact. For what felt like hours, she endured his abuse as he tortured her body physically and sexually, not giving her a single second to catch her breath. The loud thud of something hitting the floor made her jolt as he pulled the vibrator out of her body, only turning it off once it was out. As clarity began to wash over her, it was immediately taken away again as he pushed his hard cock deep inside of her.

With no way to fight back or move her body, she naturally began to clench around him. Elena's body contracted and surged as he thrust his cock into her deeply and repeatedly. Suddenly feeling a wave of terror wash over her, she couldn't remember the last time she took a breath as he continued to push through her. As her vision began to go white, every nerve was on the verge of bursting, and the only thing she could hear was her deafening heartbeat, echoing through her bones like shockwaves. She tried to scream out for help, but there was no air to carry it. As she closed her eyes in defeat, a cascade of fireworks began to explode throughout her body, suddenly awake, she could hear screaming all around her, her lungs bursting with fresh air as she felt her body melting.

David removed her blindfold first, then Elena watched David unbuckle her wrists and said. "I feel like I peed myself. Did you hear that screaming?" David didn't respond. "Am I bleeding?" Again, he didn't respond. He easily picked her up and laid her on the bed. As he carried her, she looked around for anything that might answer her questions. "Why aren't you answering me?" she asked as she began to cry. Why wouldn't he answer her? David held her tightly, as she stared at him. "Am I dead?" She asked. David chuckled, "There she is, no you're not dead." Elena let out a relieved sigh. "Why didn't you answer me before?" she asked, holding his cheek. David was confused, "You haven't asked me anything, you were just babbling incoherently," he said, furrowing his eyebrows.

Elena laid there confused for nearly an hour as her body continued to tingle, holding David as he gently caressed her. "We should probably go see the others, they might start to worry," she suggested. He nodded his head, helping her stand up. After washing herself off, she went downstairs. Jennifer and Tiffany were smiling as they sat at the dinner table. "You guys are still eating?" she asked. Jennifer laughed as Summer responded. "You haven't been gone that long." Elena looked at the clock and gasped as she realized, she had only just arrived home about an hour and a half ago. "What the fuck just happened to me?" she wondered. David joined the group while they ate dinner. As they talked, Elena learned that she was in fact screaming obscenities toward the end, something she didn't realize, but Summer and Tiffany confirmed as they could hear her downstairs.

The next morning, David woke up, Jennifer clinging to him as she slept. After getting out of bed, he went downstairs to find Tiffany making breakfast. "Is everybody awake?" he asked. "Not yet, but I think Elena's at work already," she answered. David slapped her hard on the ass before grabbing his coffee cup. "I want you to start testing the boys until you find their aptitude level, forget about lesson plans for now, all we need is for them to pass a high school equivalency." "What about College?" she asked. David shook his head. "There is no college, they need to learn life skills, something tangible," he said as he poured his coffee. "What do we do about school, if they already know enough to pass their tests?" she asked, pressing her body against him seductively. "You want me to tell you?" he asked, gripping the front of her neck. "Yes sir," she moaned. "Read to them, and have them read to you, aloud, whenever possible. There needs to be rewards for seeking knowledge," he insisted. "Are they ever going to go to school?" she asked. "Yes, when they have enough self-control, I don't want them influenced or misled by others," he said quietly as he leaned in to kiss her.

"Good morning," Summer said as she walked into the kitchen. "Good morning, is Jennifer awake?" he asked, letting go of Tiffany. "She was in the bathroom when I came down," she responded. As the three sat down to eat breakfast, Jennifer walked in the kitchen, hair disheveled, pouring a cup of coffee. "Good morning Master," she said. "Good morning, how's it going with the dog hunt?" he asked. "I'm still waiting for some responses," she answered. Jennifer sat in David's lap with her coffee. "Since all of my baby-mamas are here, I'll tell you what I think," he said, receiving side-eyed looks from the girls. "With what I've seen, I suspect my children are going to come out precooked. There might not be very much we can teach them, so we need to be sure they can cope with what they already know. Not only are they going to be involved in our plan, but they will be the future of our family, so they need to be prepared."

Jennifer set her coffee down, turning and straddling David in his chair. "Are you paying attention?" he asked Jennifer. "I am, they're the future of our family," she said as she kissed him deeply on the mouth. Summer and Tiffany watched wide eyed as Jennifer tried to slide her shirt off her shoulders while her tongue pulled at the inside of his lips. Pushing her back by her shoulders, he tried to continue. "Just assume they'll have to start from scratch, what do they need to know, and can they build a family with nothing," he said before Jennifer interrupted him again, this time putting her nipple in his mouth. Summer leaned over to

Tiffany and whispered, "I think she's going to try and fuck him." Tiffany nodded her head, "Sure looks like it."

Pushing her back again and lifting her shirt, he continued. "Ahem, I doubt they're any kind of prodigy, but maybe this gives us a little head start, so let's not waste the opportunity." Summer and Tiffany nodded their heads as Jennifer, who had pulled David's pajama pants down at this point, guided his cock inside of her. "Jennifer, do you have any questions?" he asked as she slowly moved her body up and down in his lap. "No Master, I think I've got it," she moaned. David clenched his teeth.

Tiffany and Summer tried not to stare as Jennifer nearly knocked David's chair backward with him in it. As she fucked David more vigorously, she reached down to play with her clit. "Fuck!" she yelled as she began cumming. Just then, the sound of footsteps running down the stairs snapped everyone out of the moment and Jennifer gripped him tightly. "Please don't move," she begged, whispering into his ear.

"Aunt Jennifer, why are you sitting in Daddy's lap," Aidan asked, sitting next to Tiffany. "I just needed a hug, I'll move in a second," she answered, still rubbing her clit. "Aidan, let's go wake up your brothers," Tiffany said, taking him upstairs. As soon as they left the table, Jennifer bit down on David's shoulder as she came all over his lap. Jennifer bit her lip as she stood up, still dripping down her thighs. "I'll go clean up," she said, fixing her panties. David shook his head, "And take a shower, you horny slut," he retorted. Pulling up his pants, he went upstairs to change. After cleaning up, he passed Tiffany on the stairs, returning to his breakfast. "I like this side of Jennifer," Summer said, putting a sausage link in her mouth. "Don't get any ideas," he said, as he started eating.

After breakfast, David spent the day unpacking his stuff and learned that the girls had been wearing his clothes in his absence, which is why some of his clothes were missing. The next two days, David went to his redeployment processing and signed out on leave that Friday at noon.

For the next four days, everyone would be home together, and that last evening after dinner, he took that opportunity to discuss his plans for the next several years. Elena, who had just learned that David was moving to Arizona after their next deployment, could not go with him unless she reenlisted for a minimum of three years, however, she had to wait one year before her contract end date to do so. "What if I reenlist and they deploy me again?" she asked. David shook his head. "You won't, all staff sergeants and sergeants first class are being sent to Arizona after the deployment," he said confidently. "Well, that only means you, I'm still just a sergeant," she explained.

David went to the kitchen to make a pot of coffee before continuing. "Master, do you know something? I thought her future was uncertain because she came with us?" Jennifer asked. "Give me a sec, I'll tell you what I know," he said. Sitting down with two cups, he handed one to Elena and began to explain. "In a month, the Brigade is going to reorganize and many of us are going to switch Battalions. I don't know if that includes you or not, but I do know that after that, I'm going to get promoted and there is a very high likelihood you will as well," he said confidently. Elena was intrigued, having experienced his predictions in the past. "When will that happen?" she asked.

"Starting in May, unless you get picked up sooner," he said. Tiffany watched the conversation with intrigue as she ate dried apples out of a bag. She had already read David's notebooks, so she wasn't surprised by his predictions, but still enjoyed watching how others reacted to it.

"So, do I just reenlist while we're deployed?" she asked. "Yes, you will still be under ten years, and this would be your last reenlistment before going indefinite," he explained. "Master, how many years are you going to reenlist for?" Jennifer asked. "My reenlistment window falls after the ten year mark, so I will be indefinite," he said, patting her head. "How long will we be in Arizona?" Summer asked. "Until I retire, which is in about seven and a half years," he answered.

After their conversation finished, Elena pulled David aside. "Can you come to my room tonight?" she asked. "Why, is there something wrong with your room?" he responded. Elena blushed timidly. Summer grabbed her shoulder, surprising her. "Shit, you scared me!" Elena shouted. "What are you trying to do?" Summer asked, squinting her eyes. "I just miss sleeping next to him," she said, dodging the question. "Hey Jennifer!" "What is it?" "Can you switch with Elena tonight?" Summer asked as she smiled at Elena. "Sure, just let me change first!" she responded. "You're welcome," she said flirtatiously as she turned to go upstairs. Elena turned back to David, who shrugged, not saying a word.

Chapter 26

Leaving Everyone Behind

The following month, David, along with many others, received orders to transfer to the other Battalion, something he expected, but to Elena's surprise, she was transferred as well. They were both assigned to the same company, consisting solely of human intelligence collection teams. For the next four months, David took charge of training for the company, something he always excelled in. He was aware that opportunities to train in the future would be side-lined for the sake of other organizations, so he didn't waste a single day. Senior leaders yielded to his requests, thankful to have someone even willing to put it all together. While Elena's admiration for him only grew, feeling a sense of ownership and privilege for being in his life.

David's professional and social behavior were dynamically different, but seamlessly fit together. His word was law, and nobody dared to question him, even his officers relied on his command presence and expertise. However, the Soldiers didn't fear him, often going out of their way to curry favor, yet wouldn't dare disobey him. After the fourth month, he was promoted to Sergeant First Class and transferred to a different company to lead a special intelligence platoon, meanwhile, she was promoted the following month and had to stay within her company, but was assigned to the Operational Management Team, because of her analytical background. Just as David predicted, training was much more difficult to plan due to the collaboration efforts made with other organizations, who only seemed interested in using his Battalion like tools or spare parts. Not allowing much time for internal training or team building.

At home, Jennifer was able to find two Dachshund puppies, which they ironically named Delilah and Jezebel. At first, only Summer and Tiffany understood why he wanted wiener dogs, but they weren't about to question his preferences. Elena would have preferred a larger dog, but after David spent more than an hour overexplaining the benefits and responsibilities of taking care of a large dog, as well as the benefits of owning dachshunds, she acquiesced. At David's request, Jennifer also contacted a legal document provider and requested a dissolution of marriage.

Last summer, the girls took the children to the water park while David was deployed, so Aidan and the other two were itching to go again. This summer, they thought they would have to convince David, so they had prepared a whole speech for presenting their request. However, to their surprise, he immediately agreed. Tiffany had managed to convince the head lifeguard to allow the boys a swim test, granting them access to other areas of the pool without direct or hands-on supervision. Lily, on the other hand, was too young, but was old enough to wear trainers. It was early June, and Brian had just turned four years old, Aidan was almost six, and little David was going to be three in three months. Lily was just over a year old, so Summer had bought her very own trainer.

As David packed the van that morning, all of the girls got ready and put the puppies in the kennel. As David drove to the water park, the girls talked amongst themselves in the back seat as Elena sat up front. "So, what do you think of Texas?" he asked. "It's really flat," she said, staring out the window. "Some parts of it are, but what else?" he persisted. "I think it's fine, but I'm not use to the humidity yet," she answered. Elena sat quietly for a moment, before asking David, "Can I ask you a sensitive question?" "Sure, ask me any question you want," he responded. "Why can't we bring family members with us?" she asked. "Do you want the official answer or the David answer?" he asked as he smiled. Elena lowered her head, "I'd like to hear the David answer," she said quietly. "I actually don't have a problem with it, but I'm not going to compete for control. This is my life, my future, and my path. If someone tries to take any part of that from me, then I will kill to protect it," he said seriously.

David clenched the steering wheel tightly. "I don't think I'm unreasonable, but I want absolute dominion and control, only then can I truly protect my family. I won't lose them again." Elena held his hand while he calmed down. "I understand why it would seem unreasonable, but I've been with you for a while, and you're a lot softer than you seem. So, what's the official answer?" she asked as she teased his hand. Kissing her hand, he said, "I don't want anyone to know what we know, or where we're going, or what we have, because as Tiffany said, there might be others, and the more inconspicuous we are, the safer we'll be."

"We're here!" Jennifer screamed. After David parked, everyone carried their stuff to the gate, as David carried the coolers, one on each shoulder, with Aidan and Brian carrying the charcoal and cooking supplies. Tiffany purchased the bands, excited as she held them out. "What is it?" David asked. "The boys don't have to take a swim test," she said excitedly. As everyone walked to the picnic site, they could actually feel onlookers burning holes through all of them. It was at this time, David recalled his first visit to the waterpark after his reset. He was utterly unimpressed with the herd of cattle gathered around the water, it was like everyone got dressed with beer goggles on and got their dieting and fitness advice from Mad magazine.

Meanwhile, their group had Tiffany, a 30 year old vixen with long legs. Summer, the 28 year old innocent girl next door. Elena, the 27 year old thin exotic beauty. Jennifer, the 26 year old curvy sweetheart. David, who is carrying a fifty pound cooler on each shoulder! What the actual fuck was up with that! Wait, even the kids are carrying shit! David smiled, even though he was protective and secretive, he quite enjoyed showing off his family. Especially his children, who, despite their age, were as strong as young adults. David put everything in their place and cleaned out the barbeque pit, while everyone downgraded to swimsuits and put on their sunblock.

Once they finished, it was a mad dash to the park, David followed the boys, while Summer followed the girls to the pool area, Lily by her side. The boys rode the tube slide while David went down the other slide, coming out near the kids pool before jumping into the swimming area. Elena grabbed him from behind, wrapping her legs around him under water as she held him like a buoy. "How long you think you could tread water with me holding onto you?" she asked. "All night if I needed to, but I'm going to have to make dinner eventually," he said. Elena rolled her eyes and kissed him. "Can we finish our conversation from earlier?" she asked in a soft voice. "Sure, let's go somewhere better to talk," he said as he swam to the ladder, Elena still clinging to him.

David made it all the way to the bottom of the stairs before Elena finally let go. Grabbing a two-person tube, they climbed to the top. "Aunt Lena, are you going to ride the tube slide?" Brian asked, as he snuck up from behind. "It certainly looks like it," she responded.

After their launch, David and Elena rode their tube like a wild bobsled down the chute, splashing with every turn and spin, until they crashed into the leisure river at the bottom. As the water settled, they both turned until their heads touched, laying back, cheek to cheek. "What else did you want to talk about?" he asked. "Not yet, let me enjoy this for a moment," she responded. As they floated down the river, she reached her arm around, holding his head close to hers. "Why do I like this so much?" she asked rhetorically. David turned his head, kissing her on the lips as the water continued to carry them around. "How much do you think it cost for each of us to join your little harem?" she asked playfully. "Probably half a million each, if everything is divided fairly," he answered. "Oh my god! Is it really that much? She asked, shocked by his answer. "Uh huh," he nodded.

"So, If I wanted to bring a family member, it would be half a million per person?" she asked. "That's what the math says," he answered. "Do you have that much money" she asked timidly. "Not yet, not enough for everyone, but everybody chips in, especially Summer," he said. "I've been able to save lots of money, thanks to you, but I don't think it's near enough," she said sadly. "Well, if you have any intention on staying, you should contribute, but you should know, Summer has agreed to cover your share, but she's also covering Jennifer and Tiffany, so if you want to pay your share fairly, then it's one quarter of what I earn, no questions, no receipts, no asking for it back," he explained. "I get it, I figured it would be that way," she said.

As they reached the stairs, they both got out and went to the main pool, joining the others. David took Lily and played with her as Summer went with the others. Why is it when women go to the pool, they just lounge around, you hardly see them actually swimming? As the girls climbed on the floating lily pads, David swam with his daughter in the deep end, keeping her within reach. Of course, the bachelors had to try their hand at least once, causing his lip to curl as he watched them get shut down one by one. That is, until Jennifer started pointing and five pairs of eyes, burning with envy, nearly blasted a hole through his brain. "Come on Lily, let's go see what kind of trouble your aunt got me into," he said as she made his way over.

"Hey, what'chu ladies talking about?" he asked. Jennifer jumped into his arms and pointed like a little girl taddling to her teacher. "Master, they wanted to know if we were here with someone, and we said yes," she said. "Is that all?" he asked. "Well, Tiffany said she was here with her ex and Summer said she was here with her fiancé, then Elena said she was here with her boyfriend, and I'm here with my husband," she responded, as if expecting praise. "So, you pointed out your husband?" he asked. "Yes, that's what I did." David smiled, kissing her and setting her up on the lily pad. One of the guys spoke, "I didn't see anybody else come in with you, so if you didn't want to be bothered, you could've just said so. You don't have to lie about being in a relationship." David grabbed Tiffany, pulling her into the water, "My girl's don't lie," he said as Tiffany held onto him.

Several hours later, David went back to the picnic table and started preparing lunch, just as a few uninvited guests arrived. David smiled, because even though he didn't particularly like outsiders, he always had a knack for hospitality. "Gentlemen, welcome, please have a seat," he gestured to the table. Looking at each other, they didn't know what to do. David then reached into his cooler and pulled five beers out of the ice and placed them on the table. "It's rude to refuse someone's hospitality," he said, gesturing to the seats. "Hey man, are they really telling the truth, or are you just protecting them?" one asked. Ignoring the question, David changed the subject, "You guys want to join us for lunch? We have brats and burgers if you're interested." Not willing to pass up the opportunity, they conceded. "Thanks man, that's really cool."

As they talked, the boys showed up, running for the cooler. "Water first, then dry yourselves off. Aiden, go get your mom and tell the rest dinner will be ready soon," he commanded. "Yes Daddy!" he responded as he ran off. "Are these all yours?" another asked. "Uh huh," he nodded his head. "Brian, you and David drag that other picnic table over here, these men are going to join us for dinner," he said, pointing at a nearby table.

The five men stared in shock as the two small boys dragged the 250 pound picnic table over, lining it up with the other. "Gentlemen, if I could have you spread out at a double arm interval, I would appreciate that, unless you want to sit on the far end," he said. The men moved apart without question, a look of fearful respect on their faces.

As the women approached, David threw them their towels. "These gentlemen are joining us for lunch, and I had them spread out, so pick a spot between them once you're dried off." Elena was confused and approached David. "You invited them to lunch?" she whispered. "No, they invited themselves, so do as I say and pick a seat," he said quietly, slapping her ass as she turned. As he served dinner, the entire group talked and shared stories, even the girls seemed to loosen up once the conversation gained momentum. David learned that all five men were in one of the Cavalry squadrons on base, though he wasn't surprised. However, these Soldiers were surprised when they learned that David was a Sergeant First Class, that Elena was a Staff Sergeant, that Summer was a Pharmacist, and that even though Tiffany and Jennifer weren't working, one was trained in animal agriculture and the other a horticulturalist.

By the time everyone finished eating, they had all forgotten about why they came over in the first place and even began speaking formally to David and the women. Once they were finished, David began cleaning, but not before telling the boys to go with their mother. Summer picked up Lily, bringing her to David for a kiss before departing, just as Brian and little David ran to Jennifer. Aiden asked his mother if he could go down the slides again, as she walked with him back to the park. Meanwhile, Elena was helping David clean as the Soldiers were obviously trying to put the pieces together.

"Sergeant Renado, so is what they said true?" one asked. David frowned. "Please, call me David, and yes, I already told you, they aren't lying," he answered calmly. The Soldiers continued talking but suddenly stopped as they watch David drag the picnic table back to its original spot, as if it were made of plastic. Noticing their expressions, Elena's penchant for drama began to itch, and she desperately wanted to scratch it. So, before leaving, she turned to David. "Sir, I want to sleep in your bed tonight, so I'm going to switch with Jennifer," she said boldly. David nodded, not looking up. "Okay, sounds like a plan," he responded. After kissing him, she turned to leave, as all five soldiers stared in disbelief. David was about to head back before turning toward them, "There's still drinks and food in the cooler, so, as long as we're here, help yourself," he said, nodding as he left.

Strangely, for the rest of their stay, all five Soldiers took on a protective role, feeling a sense of responsibility toward the girls and his children, never daring to show an inappropriate amount of familiarity. As David's group left, he met the same Soldiers in the parking lot, shaking their hands and wishing them well, even the girls, with the exception of Summer shook their hands.

On the way back, Jennifer turned to David. "Master, why did you invite them for lunch?" she asked. David smiled before responding, "They were actually coming over to start shit, I think, so I changed the circumstances of their visit, and now we have allies, at least a little bit." Tiffany leaned forward and kissed him on the back of the neck. "You aren't supposed to use your powers for evil sir," she teased.

At the end of the following month, David and Jennifer's divorce was finalized and when they got their documents, she decided to move out, even though he had to wait thirty days before getting remarried. Once she moved her stuff out, Summer immediately moved in, despite not yet being married. As far as Summer was concerned, the waiting period wasn't her fault, and neither Tiffany nor Jennifer could argue. After the waiting period, David took Summer to the Justice of the Peace with Elena and Jennifer, while Tiffany stayed at home with the children.

Once they got home, rather than celebrating, Summer called a meeting with the girls. "Where is David, is he not going to be a part of this?" Elena asked. "No, this doesn't really concern him, even though it's about him," Summer replied. Tiffany and Jennifer didn't say anything, curious as to why Summer wanted to have a meeting in the first place. "Now that David and I are married, I don't want anyone else sleeping in his bed, at least until he deploys," she demanded. "So, we can't have sex with him for the next month and a half?" Jennifer asked. "I don't think that's what she meant," Tiffany corrected. "Are you allowed to make that demand?" Elena wondered. "That's why I wanted to have a meeting. Tiffany got to marry him first, so there was no competition, plus I had just graduated from college when Jennifer married him. However, now I'm here, and I feel like I've waited long enough," she stated bluntly. "So, we can still have sex?" Jennifer asked excitedly. Summer sighed, "Yes, you can still have sex. I couldn't take that from you if I tried," she said.

Tiffany agreed, feeling responsible for keeping order amongst the girls, even though she didn't like the request. "I've never considered myself greater than any one of you, which is why I want you to accept this request. Plus, it's because of my job that we can live in this house and you two can stay home with the children, so I think I've earned that right," Summer said. "Can we at least have one day in the last week?" Tiffany asked, hopefully. "Yes, I suppose that's also fair," Summer answered. "While we're here, would it be appropriate to establish a chain of command or something?" Elena asked. Jennifer and Summer looked at Tiffany. "I suppose that wouldn't be the worst idea, especially if there's going to be more of us," Summer said cautiously.

Tiffany took out David's book and let out a deep sigh. "As far as I know, David has only been in love with one person, so it's safe to assume we won't be the last," she said as she opened the book. "His wife?' Elena assumed. "No, believe it or not, it was someone he never actually met in person. I don't know what kind of influence she had on him, but losing her really messed him up," Tiffany said solemnly. "Are you saying he doesn't love us?" Elena asked. "No, I know he does, because I feel it, but I do know it wasn't easy for me, or any of us for that matter," she said seriously.

"Well, it was you three that took me in and took care of me. Honestly, I can't imagine how miserable I would have been if I decided to stay, So I have no desire to put myself ahead of any of you," Elena said. "I don't think we're going to compete with each other over who gets to be in charge, but I like Jennifer's idea of Tiffany being the Matriarch. I know she sacrifices a lot for us, so we should support her," Summer added.

When their block leave ended, Elena and David had already sent their equipment ahead and only carried a few bags with them, to include their weapons. The morning of their departure, after telling everyone goodbye, companies lined up to receive their boarding passes. Of course, the Battalion staff and commanders were seated in business class, while everyone else was seated randomly throughout the plane.

David was assigned 27J, which was a window seat on the right side of the plane. As David stowed his bag in the overhead compartment, he heard a familiar voice. "Excuse me, would you mind switching seats with me?" she asked. David turned to see Elena negotiating with his neighbor, a Sergeant from one of the other companies. "What seat are you assigned?" he asked. Elena held out her boarding pass. "23F, it's a front row seat," she said as she pointed. He didn't even hesitate grabbing his stuff, rushing to take his new seat.

David shook his head. "You are really something else," he said as he stepped toward her. "How about you take the window," he said as he gestured to his seat. Elena smiled, touching his hand as she passed him, taking his place. David sat in the aisle seat and buckled his seatbelt, holding onto Elena's hand as they waited for takeoff. The entire flight, she never left his side. "I hope we're close," she said as she slowly closed her eyes. He honestly had no idea where she was going, but because his ranking was highest amongst his peers, he did manage to take charge of the first platoon in his company, rather than the fifth, like last time.

Chapter 27

At Least for Now

David spent the first two weeks training in Kuwait, before their teams would be sent to their area of operation, however, he knew the first team would be operating out of the Victory Base Complex, sticking close to the command group. Additionally, Elena's Operational Management Team also operated out of the same area, coordinating collection efforts in the south, while the other Battalion operated in the north. News about David's divorce had spread within the company and even though he had remarried a month prior, this side of the story wasn't known within his organization. So naturally, when others saw David and Elena together, they just assumed she was pining to take that position.

Had it not been for David's professionalism and effective leadership skills, his Commander or First Sergeant might have discouraged him, however, neither one had any intention of interfering with his personal affairs. With so many other issues to worry about, they thought it was best to enable him, rather than hinder him. His commander, Captain Anna Ortiz, a 26 year old graduate of A&M University, was a Texan by birth and tended to play favorites. Additionally, his candid personality, in conjunction with his unusually high degree of experience made her feel comfortable having him around. His First Sergeant, Sergeant First Class Robert Harper, a 36 year old analyst from

Philadelphia, was a baseball fan, smoker, and avid coffee drinker. Even though David wasn't a baseball fan, he was a smoker and coffee drinker, which was enough to cultivate a symbiotic social comradery.

One aspect of deployment David didn't miss was the relief and transfer of authority, a process that was both unnecessarily micromanaged and overly redundant. However, David kept his expertise close to the chest for the time being, not wanting to seem arrogant, even though his Lieutenant knew he was holding back. When assigned rooms, David was not special. For those lucky enough to have sleeping quarters, rather than tents, a roommate was inevitable, and his roommate was one of his Company's fellow Signals Intelligence collectors, a Sergeant First class that he was friendly with, even in his last life their wives were friends. However, this time, because he did not allow his girls to get involved with the family readiness group, their interactions were less frequent.

David did bring Jennifer to several events, to include hail and farewell gatherings, formal organizational events, and ceremonies. But when it came to family events, such as Company picnics, organization day events, as well as holiday parties, he brought everyone. Even though nobody was fully aware of his relationship with the others, and no one found proof of impropriety in his actions, Soldiers in his Company still sarcastically assigned him the moniker, Sultan. A nickname that even circulated around the rest of the Battalion and even some of the local nationals. However, most of these people surmised that it was because of his language proficiency and dominant personality, especially since he always seemed to find himself working alone, which was misunderstood by several leaders.

One consequence of his team being co-located with the command group was that his team leader always took over as the acting commander whenever she had to travel around the battlefield, leaving him without a lieutenant. Another cause was his education and experience. Missions and tasks seldom came when they were convenient and because David spent more time in his team room than his quarters, he was often immediately available when tasks and missions were given to his team. "Sergeant Sultan, is your interpreter here?" David sighed. "Yes, as a matter of fact, I keep him tied up under my desk like a gimp for just such an occasion. No, why the hell would he be here in the middle of the night!" he answered sarcastically. "Let me see what you got. I'll translate this real quick and get it back to you in a few minutes." "Sergeant Sultan, the HCT brought in a guest, you think you can have your team check his phone while he's here?" they asked. "They're doing something at the moment, I'll just clone the data and send you the copy once it's done," he answered.

The operational unit's Battalion staff received more reports from him directly than his team as a whole, bolstering his reputation. Additionally, every time he submitted a report anywhere, he updated his action report to his parent command and sent a draft copy of the intelligence report to the OMT, which were coincidently reviewed by Elena. "Chief, I got another intelligence report from Sergeant Renado. So, I'm going to go talk to him about some of the issues I found," Elena said, grabbing her hat and carbine. "Sure, while you're there, can you ask him for one of those bottles of iced tea?" he responded. It took Elena fifteen minutes to reach his team room, which was considerably closer than either of their living quarters, so they would often spend time there.

"David, I found some issues with your report," she announced as she barged in. "Impossible, It's a draft report and you know I don't ghost-write reports, so what you got is what I got," he responded dismissively. "I know, I just wanted an excuse to see you," she said, kissing his cheek. David was making a slideshow of his findings to give to the Battalion staff when she interrupted him, so he quickly finished and emailed it out. As soon as he sent the email, he turned around to see Elena snooping through his refrigerator. "Are you hungry, or does chief want another tea," he asked. "Both," Elena said, pulling out a bottle of tea and a protein bar. David made iced tea nearly every week, using the free one liter water bottles, as well as sugar and tea from the Post Exchange nearby. Many thought this was a side hustle he had developed, but was actually something he started last time when he was in a more remote operating base. Despite this, he had no shame in using this as leverage for building rapport, and Elena knew this all too well.

"David, what would you do if either one of us didn't have a roommate?" she asked, pushing his laptop aside. "I think I'd be spending a lot more time convincing you that we shouldn't be fucking in our hooch," he answered. Elena set her weapon aside, then sat on his desk, pulling him close to her. "I know, but I like having you to myself like this," she said, wrapping her legs around him. David pulled her off the table and into his lap, catching her off guard. "How much longer are you going to be here?" she asked, pressing her head into his. "Probably until midnight, unless we get a mission," he answered quietly. "Are we going to get hit tonight?" she wondered. David thought for a minute. "I don't think so, but I'm honestly not sure, I wasn't here last time," he replied. "You weren't?" she asked, surprised. "No, last time I was on an operating base near Amara in the south."

Elena kissed David long on the lips, pushing her tongue into his mouth as he pulled her face tightly into his, causing her to gasp. After several long minutes, she leaned back. "Fuck!" she exclaimed. "What is it?" he asked. "I have to get back," she sighed, grabbing her weapon. "Don't forget your snack," he said, holding up the protein bar. "Thanks," she grunted, snatching it from his hand, then slamming the door on her way out. David merely shrugged, opening up his laptop. Later that night, as David stepped outside for a cigarette, he saw the Battalion S2, Captain Small, an ironic name for a man as big as he. "Good evening sir, why are you here so late?" David asked. "I could ask you the same thing," he responded. David shrugged.

Captain Small was throwing knives at a dart board David made from a pallet and reinforced with wood, hanging on a concrete barrier. "How long does it take to get good at this?" he asked. David watched as the knives bounced off the target, clanging against the ground. "Not long, but you have to be consistent," David said. Captain Small handed the knives to David. "Show me," he said. David stood about ten feet away and as he explained the steps, threw three knives, one after the other, hitting the target's center. "Master your half-spin throw before changing it up, it should feel natural every time," David said, retrieving the knives. As he walked back, he shifted one knife to his left hand before turning quickly, sinking three knives in the target in rapid succession.

The next morning, David was eating breakfast when Elena joined him at the table. "Good morning," he said, not looking up. "Look, I'm sorry about last night," she said timidly. "It's just, I was really horny, and I wanted," David reached out and covered her mouth. "Would you keep your voice down! People might hear you." Elena licked the inside of his hand, causing him to pull it away quickly. "I want your dick inside of me Sergeant Sultan," she said unabashedly. "Ha ha, very funny," he responded. David finished his breakfast and before he left, Elena pulled him close, "I meant what I said," she whispered.

A couple months later, David was on his fifth month of deployment, when he was preparing to go home on leave. David led a seven person team and with his Lieutenant, decided to offer first pick for time off to his most junior Soldiers, while he picked the least favorable, the first opening, just as he had done before. Unsurprisingly, Elena had done the same. As he was preparing his Daily situation report, the Lieutenant and First Sergeant walked in. "Hey Renado, come outside for a smoke," his First Sergeant said. "Sure," he said as he stood up. Outside, the three of them smoked while playing with the throwing knives. "Is there a reason you came by?" David asked. "Nah, I just hate staying cooked up in that office all day. Plus, you motherfuckers are more fun to hang out with," he answered.

As they continued to bullshit, one of David's Soldiers, Specialist Pike, brought two cups of coffee out, giving one to David, and the other to First Sergeant Harper. "Thanks Pike," David said, as if he was expecting it. "Sergeant, you've got your

Soldiers bringing you coffee?" the First Sergeant asked. David shook his head. "They do that on their own," the Lieutenant interjected. As they were talking, Captain small joined them. "Good morning gentlemen," he said as he sat down. "Do you need something from us, sir?" David asked. Captain Small rubbed the back of his head. "Actually, I need this translated and typed out, but my interpreter, says he can't type in Arabic." David took the paper. "I call bullshit, but it's simple, tell him he can either type this out in the air conditioned office, or go with us on our mission shortly while our interpreter types it out instead," he said, handing the paper back. First Sergeant Harper looked at David with a concerned expression. "You guys have a mission?" he asked. David shook his head, "No, they're just going to take the vehicles in for maintenance, but he doesn't know that." Captain Small laughed as he walked back to his office.

As the three continued to chat, Elena walked into the office, then immediately walked out, noticing David on the picnic table. "Good morning Sergeant McKeen," The lieutenant said. "Good morning everyone," she responded respectfully. As she sat down, the Lieutenant stood, heading back into the office. "So, I heard you and Renado go back a ways," First Sergeant Harper said, taking a sip of his coffee. "Yes, we met in language school, and we've been close ever since," she answered. "How has his team been for the OMT?" he asked. Elena fought the urge to gush as she tried to find the best answer. "Their intelligence reports are really thorough, and the chief still holds a grudge for taking him from us," she responded jokingly. As the First Sergeant stood up, he handed the empty cup to David, before heading out. "Have fun on leave," he said as he left. Elena leaned close. "I can't wait to get you home and into a real bed," she said seductively.

That next week, David and Elena finally arrived, luckily their house wasn't far away, so David waited until they landed before texting Tiffany. As they walked out of the small airport, Summer met them in the terminal, jumping at David like one of those sticky wall crawlers you buy out of a gumball machine. As the three of them descended the escalator, Summer still attached, they could hear Jennifer's shrieking downstairs. "Master, you're home, you're home!" she said, jumping as she skipped toward him. Setting Summer down, he picked up Jennifer, kissing her like they were being photographed for a calendar. After reaching the van, still parked on the curb, David put the bags in the back as the rest got inside. As soon as David hopped in the passenger seat, Tiffany pulled his head to her, kissing him fiercely in front of everyone.

After everyone got home, David immediately went upstairs to take a shower. As the water fell on his face, he heard the door open, then close again. Not bothering to investigate, he simply continued showering. As the water rained down from above, two hands wrapped around his stomach, as a thin body pressed against his back. "I guess I should have asked if you wanted a shower first," he said as he turned around. Elena held his body tightly as she kissed him under the water. "How did you know it was me?" she asked. "I can't answer that without insulting you," he answered. Looking down, she sighed. "It's okay, I may not have big tits, but I've got you now, and that's good enough," she said, wrapping one leg around him.

David gripped her neck firmly, pushing her leg down. "No, you don't, not yet." Elena frowned, "Are you mad at me?" she asked. He shook his head. "No, but Summer gets dibs, it's her privilege as my wife," he answered. Elena was disappointed, but didn't argue. "At least let me wash you off before you tend to her, but I want some too," she said as she began washing him. Meanwhile, Summer sat in her room, waiting for David on the floor with nothing on but her silver choker, listening to the conversation coming from the bathroom. As David came out of the shower, he noticed Summer sitting on his bedroom floor, tears running down her cheeks. "Why are you crying?" he asked. Summer sniffled, still unwilling to look up. "Am I a good wife?" she asked. David thought before answering. "Where is this coming from all of a sudden?" he asked, sitting on the bed.

David watched as Summer crawled toward him, kissing and rubbing her tears on his feet. "I love you, and I'll do anything for you. I'll be anything you want if that makes me a good wife." David grinned as he reached down to grab a fist full of her hair, tugging slightly as she stood. "So, you'll do anything for me, huh?" Summer nodded, a desperate look in her eyes. After smacking her face, he doubled down. "Anything?" he asked again. "Yes sir," she said, her voice shaking. Pushing her to the ground, he leaned over. "What does that make you?" he asked in a stern voice. "Yours sir?" David smacked her again. "What are you?" he asked even louder. "I'm your property sir," she cried, desperation in her voice. David smacked her again. "If you're my property, then what does that make me?" he asked. "Master, please. Let me worship you, I promise to be a good wife," she begged. David stood upright. "You are a stubborn pain in the ass." Summer nodded her head. "Yes Master."

David lifted her by the neck and put her down on the bed. Leaning close, he growled. "But you're my stubborn pain in the ass. And remember, your body is my playground, and I intend to use you until there's nothing left." Summer looked up at him as he continued to hold her. "Yes Master. Please fuck me like a whore, I want you to use me," she whimpered. David picked up his phone and after sending a text, set his phone down, turning back to Summer. "Scoot back and spread your legs, I don't want you to move until I tell you," he commanded. "Yes master," she responded.

Seconds later, Jennifer was standing at his door, hands folded in front of her. "Master, you called for me?" Jennifer said, a smile on her face. Gesturing to Summer he ordered, "Make her cum." Jennifer didn't hesitate, immediately dropping her clothes on the floor, she grabbed the double ended vibrator from the nightstand and climbed onto the bed. With a determined expression on her face, Summer didn't move or say a word as Jennifer carefully inserted the toy inside of herself. Now, perfectly positioned to fuck Summer, Jennifer leaned down and whispered in Summer's ear. David watched curiously as Summer nodded, while Jennifer reached down to turn on the vibrator.

Summer's face immediately went from determined to shock as her eyes rolled back, biting her lip. Meanwhile, Jennifer began moving her hips as she teased Summer's nipples with her tongue. Within a minute, Jennifer began to tremble as she shouted, "Now, cum now!" Summer let out a deep breath as she came violently on Jennifer, gushing onto the bed. David's lips curled as he watched Jennifer chuckling on top of Summer's limp body, still twitching. "Now, hold her," he ordered. Jennifer removed the toy and dropped it to the floor after turning it off, then sat behind Summer, holding her between her legs as he mounted her on the bed. David fucked Summer nonstop for several hours, as Jennifer held her. If David was the Dominant aggressor, Jennifer was her submissive support, kissing her and holding her gently as he ravaged her lower body. Even when Summer fainted, he didn't stop, occasionally causing her to wake up mid orgasm, disoriented and moaning.

As Summer opened her eyes, she looked up to see David's face, inches from hers. The room was pitch black and Jennifer was nowhere to be found. Turning to check her phone, she noticed the time, it was almost 2:00am and the whole house was asleep. Sneaking out of bed, she walked to the bathroom, expecting to find a disheveled mess looking back at her, but was surprised at what she saw in the mirror. Other than pillow prints on her face, she looked youthful, and her eyes even appeared to reflect a deeper blue. After checking all the rooms, she checked on Lily, kissing her in her bed before going downstairs for a drink of water.

As she stood in the kitchen drinking her water, the blue moonlight reflected off of her pale naked body. "Good morning," David said, making her jump. "I thought you were asleep," she said, catching her breath. David approached her cupping her cheek in his hand as he looked her in the eyes. "How am I supposed to sleep when my wife isn't in bed with me?" he asked quietly, kissing her gently on the lips. Summer could feel her body melting in his arms as he held her. "At least for now," she mumbled, holding onto him. David traced his finger along the sterling choker. "No, ever since I put this on your neck and long after we're both gone," he whispered softly. Summer kissed him again. "Take me to bed Master," she purred as she buried her head in his chest. David picked her up like a princess, and carried her back upstairs.

Chapter 28

The Way You Make Me Feel

Elena moaned as she bit down on David's belt. "You need to be quiet, unless you want us to get caught," he whispered as he came inside of her, her knees buckling as she held onto the wall. "I'll be fine, just give me a minute," she said, breathing deeply. David grabbed his weapon and belt, then kissed the side of her cheek.

After leaving the bathroom, he joined his First Sergeant in the chow line. "I'm back now, thanks for holding my spot," he said. Several minutes later, as David, his First Sergeant and others ate lunch, Elena joined them. "Sergeant McKeen, good to see you again," First Sergeant Harper said. "Thanks, I probably shouldn't have ran over, now I'm all hot and sweaty," she said smirking. "Renado, how come you eat the same thing every day?" First Sergeant Harper asked, pointing at his plate. David shrugged his shoulders. "I didn't realize I did that," he answered.

It had been almost nine months since David's return and the entire brigade was in Kuwait, preparing to fly back home. Once they finally landed, David knew he couldn't simply hide in the background since he had long since built a reputation within his Battalion, and his relationships with his seniors, peers, and juniors had grown beyond a simple work relationship. Especially with his command team, his former classmates, his roommate and his own team.

As David went to meet his family, Summer clung to him, kissing him deeply as he held her. With Summer in his arms, First Sergeant Harper approached. "Renado, is this your family?" he asked, looking at Summer and the children. "Yes First Sergeant, this is my wife Summer." Interrupting him, First Sergeant Harper interjected, "You can just call me Robert, unless we're at work," he said candidly. David nodded. "Then the same goes to you," he responded. "Anyway, this is my wife Summer, and our daughter Lily. You remember Jennifer, and our boys David and Brian. And this beautiful woman is Tiffany, and our son Aidan." Robert shook their hands politely, completely overlooking the significance of what he had just heard.

On the ride home, Tiffany and Jennifer were excitedly discussing their plans for block leave as Summer drove the van. After reaching home, Tiffany went upstairs to run a bath and the boys carried David and Elena's bags into the house, immediately breaking everything down and putting the dirty clothes in the laundry. Everyone took turns giving David a proper welcome, other than Elena, who simply went upstairs to take a shower in the other bathroom. "We've been looking at houses in Arizona," Summer said as she let the dogs out of the kennel. "What did you find?" he asked, holding Lily. "Our best option is to buy a house, but it's really expensive," she answered. David kissed her cheek. "Don't worry about that right now, I trust you. So, let's have a meeting about it at dinner," he said, setting Lily back down.

Tiffany grabbed him from behind, wrapping her arms around his body. "Sir, I ran a bath for you," she said quietly as she laid her head on his back. David smiled, turning to kiss her on the lips. "Thank you," he responded. Then, without giving

Summer a moment to prepare herself, he picked her up, throwing her over his shoulder before heading upstairs. After setting her down, he immediately removed her clothes, never once asking her permission or opinion. Summer watched as he undressed, then obediently followed him into the tub. For the next half hour, she sat in the tub, resting her back against him, as he held her in the water, nearly putting her to sleep as he gently scrubbed her body with the sponge.

Later that evening, as everyone ate dinner, Summer talked about the house she was looking at, even showing pictures. It was six bedrooms, six bathrooms and more than four thousand square feet, but it was five hundred fifty thousand dollars, plus it was going to need some changes and updates. "So, what do you think about the house?" Summer asked. David examined the pictures carefully before answering. "Call the agent and let them know we'll buy it outright on one condition, they are going to have to replace and repaint a lot of doors, walls and tiles. Have them send a full picture of each and every wall, floor and ceiling. We will identify the areas to work on and if they agree, we'll sign a contract for the work and pay for the house immediately, but I want a response by Monday night," he said.

Elena was surprised by his dismissive attitude concerning money, as well as Jennifer and Tiffany's lack of response to his statement. David took out his notebook and reviewed his log. According to his notes, which of course were written in code, Elena's contributions were just over fifty-six thousand, which was closer to forty percent since her arrival. Summer's contributions were just over one hundred sixty thousand, and his were just over two hundred twenty thousand. This left them with close to seven thousand dollars per month, to cover rent and living expenses. Meanwhile, David's investments have turned his nearly four hundred forty thousand into just over three million dollars over the past twelve years.

After hearing David's explanation, she stopped worrying about his ability to handle their money, and even considered giving him more. "What are we going to do with the house when we leave?" she asked. "We'll sell it," he answered without looking up. "I need one of you to find me a few contractors and engineers by next week," he said as he flipped through his book. "What kind?" Summer asked. "I need an excavation contractor that has an explosive license and access to heavy digging equipment. I also need a highway engineer and a concrete contractor and an engineer that specializes in commercial properties," he explained. "I can start looking Master," Jennifer said, writing on a sheet of paper. "Tiffany, we're going to apply for a business license and zoning permits, so you can start on that," he said handing her a note. "Sir, when do we need this?" she asked. "As soon as possible, I need them to buy fuel tanks by next year," he answered.

As the girls wrote down their assignments, Elena looked on in amazement. "You guys are something else. Is there anything I can do?" she asked, not wanting to be left out. David smiled, handing her a list. "Once we get our license and zoning permit, we're going to need these." Elena looked over the list, unsure if he was being serious. "Am I reading this right? Is that eight fifty kilogram propane tanks?" she asked, pointing to the top of the list. David took the list from her and looked at it before handing it back. "No, that's supposed to be 50k gallons. I want eight fifty-thousand gallon propane tanks, three twenty-thousand gallon petroleum tanks and seventy-four five-thousand gallon water tanks. Elena nearly fell out of her chair. "Where the fuck are you going to put these?" she asked. "I'm going to bury them," he responded.

During his redeployment block leave, after contacting the necessary people, he made a deal for the land he was prospecting. This land remained on the market for so long, because of its undesirable location and distance from any major city and open water source, but David didn't care. He purchased the 35-acre plot for only 42 thousand dollars on the spot. Meanwhile, Summer was able to negotiate for the house, but the extra work would take several months and would cost them an additional four thousand dollars.

It took Jennifer several weeks to find an excavation team willing to work in the area, especially with what he wanted done. He wanted 85 thousand cubic yards of excavation completed within the year, slightly larger than a football field, but 35 feet deep, at the bottom of the valley, including drainage holes and ditches. After paying a consultation fee, he was able to meet with him along with two other people, a highway engineer and a concrete contractor and engineer.

With the three men, he discussed his vision and even provided a sketch of his plans. The excavation team was going to work in three phases, before, during and after the engineer and concrete team finished their work. The highway engineer was requested because David felt his project was too massive in scale to rely on standard subgrade, so he insisted the three teams work together to complete his project.

The excavation foreman, who was concerned about David's ability to pay for the work, demanded half the payment up front. David agreed, even promising to pay the engineer and concrete contractor a deposit, however, he required regular updates to their work via email and detailed inspections to include pictures after each phase. With that, David wrote three checks, one for four hundred fifteen thousand dollars, and the other two for three hundred thousand each, promising to pay the rest monthly, as soon as the work started. The men were initially skeptical, but promised to deliver as soon as the first check cleared. They had one year to complete the work, but understood they would have to return again. Additionally, in order to guarantee future business, David demanded absolute discretion. As far as they were concerned, these men were going to be building a factory.

In the last few weeks, everybody's focus was on moving. Nearly every staff sergeant and sergeant first class was reassigned to the training installation in Arizona, leaving very little to do at work until their departure. Since their arrival in Arizona, David and Elena spent most of their time at work observing training and assisting the instructor cadre in grading reports and papers, as they were not allowed to interact with the trainees. At least not until they completed their new recruit cadre training, and even though they couldn't teach until they got their instructor badge, were able to observe training within the classrooms.

During this time, David had received several updates via email from the contractors, after they started working on his project back in Texas.

Update 1. 22 February. It took us several months to get the blasting permits, but we've already started drilling the holes for blasting. We should be able to start excavating by early next week. Reply to (Update 1). Don't rush, we have plenty of time, but if you get a chance, can you blast a large section in the southwest and northeast corner of the property as well, I'm going to have some wells drilled and I'd like to bury the pumps.

Update 2. 3 March. Excavation starts today. It took us a few days longer than expected to get the equipment, but we should be able to get the excavation done in about a month, including the well sites. However, I forgot to ask, but did you want to keep all of the excavated material on site? Reply to (Update 2). 4 March. Yes, just keep all of the dirt there, it's all going to get backfilled anyway. Also, if there are any trees or shrubs in the excavation or dump sites, just have them removed, I plan on landscaping once the ground is leveled out.

Update 3. 12 April. We've gotten all of the dirt moved, but in the process, we dug up several large boulders, so we just put them aside for now. Do you have a use for them? Reply to (Update 3). 14 April. I'm going to need venting and maintenance hatches, so if we can use any of them as covers or if it's possible to drill them for that, that would be cool. Reply to (Reply Update 3). I'm picking up what you're putting down, we'll take care of it.

Update 4. 27 April. We just finished dumping the subgrade, it took 160 tons of sand and about 40 tons of rock, this should keep your foundation from cracking, even if it floods. Reply to (Update 4). I should have another drilling team out there soon, they're going to drill two wells. So, make sure they get the plumbing for each well run to the site. I want those pipes buried deep as well.

Update 5. 17 May. We've started building the concrete forms for the foundation. The well drillers didn't finish the job, they said something about needing a well house for the pumps. I figured, since we're already here, we can just drop in some eight foot premade concrete tubes with an access hatch. Reply to (Update 5). 18 May. That would be awesome, as long as the pump house is set ten feet below the original ground level. Also, if you can make sure they install a hand pump at each well as a backup, I would appreciate that.

Update 6. 8 June. We finished the footers. There's enough rebar in these to build a prison. Also, as per your request, all of the concrete forms have been agitated, so, these should be stronger than granite. We should be ready to build the walls once the concrete is set. Reply to (Update 6). Cool, when you pour the walls, make sure there's holes for plumbing on each structure, as well as two foot concrete tubes for maintenance access running from each structure to the main structure. It should be in the notes I sent.

Update 7. 14 June. We've started building the forms for the walls, but the supplier said it's going to take some time to get more concrete material for this job, just an FYI.

Update 8. 20 July. We were able to start pouring the walls today, but we're going to have to come back with more concrete. Also, we're able to get a crane, so the three story bunker will have the floors poured separately and dropped in, it'll be solid though. Reply to (Update 8). That works for me, as long as the slab is smooth once it's done. Also, make sure the middle level has a one hundred fifteen by fifty foot sump on the side closest the smaller bunkers, and make sure there is enough support underneath to hold two thousand tons of water.

Update 9. 9 August. We finished the walls, and the excavation team has already started backfilling the spaces in between, after they ran the plumbing. We're going to start pouring the slabs for the caps, but apparently we're supposed to be waiting for a delivery first? Reply to (Update 9). Yes, I have several tanks that need to be installed, but you can finish the caps and close everything off for now. We'll just have to remove them for the installation once the tanks are delivered. Reply to (Reply Update 9). We can do that, just let us know when their coming in.

Update 10. 25 August. We got the caps finished today, and the sight is secure. So, once your tanks come in, just let us know and we'll come back out with the cranes.

David just got home with Elena when Summer rushed to meet him at the door. "Someone's excited to see me," he said, catching her in the air. Summer chuckled. "I don't know if anyone told you, but I kinda like you," she said, kissing him deeply. After setting her down, he walked into the living room, where Tiffany was playing with the children and picked her up, slinging her over his shoulder. "Ooh! Where are we going?" she asked. David slapped her hard on the ass. "Shut up," he replied, as he carried her upstairs.

After throwing her on the bed, he shut the door and removed his uniform, while Tiffany watched in anticipation. "I was in the middle of play…" David grabbed her chin as she spoke, "I told you to shut up," he growled. Gripping her by the neck, he pushed her down to the bed and took her pants off with one hand as he held her down with the other. Tiffany squirmed as he removed her pants. "Stop, I don't want to do this right now," she said, pushing his hands away. David smacked her cheek and pulled off her panties as she continued to fight him. "Let me go or I'm going to scream," she demanded, kicking her feet. David smacked her again, grabbing her hair before gagging her with her own panties.

Holding her hair firmly, he pulled her face close to his. "You're going to keep your mouth shut, unless you want me to hurt you," he growled as he squeezed her neck. Grabbing his belt, he tied her forearms together and pushed her over on the bed, kicking her feet apart. Tiffany's muffled screams never made it past the door as he slapped her ass, each time harder than the last. When she finally stopped, he gripped her hair tightly and slid his cock inside of her. Unable to fight back, Tiffany could only lie there and take it. Every time she tried to move her body, he would yank her hair. Every time she moved her legs, he slapped her ass. Fucking her so hard, that the bed was nearly pushed against the other wall. As he came, he thrust so hard that she involuntarily screamed through her gag.

Tiffany laid there motionless as David backed up, admiring her limp body. Tiffany stood up and turned around, an intense look in her eyes. "What?" he asked unconcerned. She spit out her underwear and effortlessly removed her arms from the belt before approaching him. "You got something to say?" he asked. Tiffany smiled. "I want to suck your cock so bad right now," she said as she grabbed his dick. David furrowed his eyebrow as she knelt down, taking his cock in her mouth. Within only a few minutes, she was back on her feet, leading him by the dick to the bed. "Fuck me again sir, I want more."

Not one to deny a lady's request, he threw her on the bed and fucked her in every conceivable position, finishing with her body nearly falling off the bed. Leaving her in a completely disheveled state. Tiffany lied next to David, resting her head on his chest as he traced his fingers down her arms. "You know sir, I love the way you make me feel," she said quietly as she kissed him. "I know you do, that's why I do it," he responded, kissing her back. "Are you happy?" he asked as he pinched her chin. Tiffany smiled. I'm probably happier than I should be," she said as she rolled on top of him. "How is that?" he asked.

Tiffany reached back, guiding his cock inside of her again. "I have a wonderful husband that takes care of me, and ouch, and lots of amazing children, plus I only had to ah, give birth to one." "I don't know why you started again if you're in so much pain," he said. "It's okay, it's just really sensitive, besides, I love fucking you," she said, wincing every time she pushed her hips back. "Also, we have such a wonderful home, and it's never lonely." "Summer has been helping out a lot with our plans, so I figured I would ask. How would you feel about a ranch?" he asked. Tiffany's eyes lit up. "Really? What kind of animals can I have?" she asked excitedly. "I was thinking about miniature cattle. Like Herefords, Highlands or Zebus," he answered. Tiffany kissed him hard. "Oh my God, I fucking love you!" she exclaimed, before wincing in pain. "I should probably wash up, I probably can't cum anymore anyway," she said as she struggled to dismount him.

That evening at dinner, Tiffany shared the news about the ranch as the others shared her excitement. "Elena, do you know what's going on with the tanks I wanted?" David asked. "Yeah, the water tanks were on back order and the propane tanks are being shipped, but the petroleum tanks require a specialist." "Well, Tiffany was able to get the license, so we just need to make a few calls. Let's try to get this done in phases, so which one can we do first?" he asked. "We can start with the water tanks the beginning of next year, and the propane tanks immediately after, but it might take a few extra months to get the petroleum tanks." After everyone finished their dinner, Summer helped David plan his next steps as Tiffany logged their progress in his notebook, using the same enigmatic code, which had ostensibly become a family practice, even his children were taught this during school.

David Renado

Tiffany Renado

Jennifer Renado

Summer Bellarose

Elena McKeen

118 ft x 82 ft
32 ft deep
2 ft thick
16 ft walls
50 ft
150 ft x 150 ft
32 ft deep
2 ft thick
26 ft walls
48 ft x 52 ft
32 ft deep
2 ft thick
16 ft walls
73 ft x 62 ft
32 ft deep
2 ft thick
16 ft walls

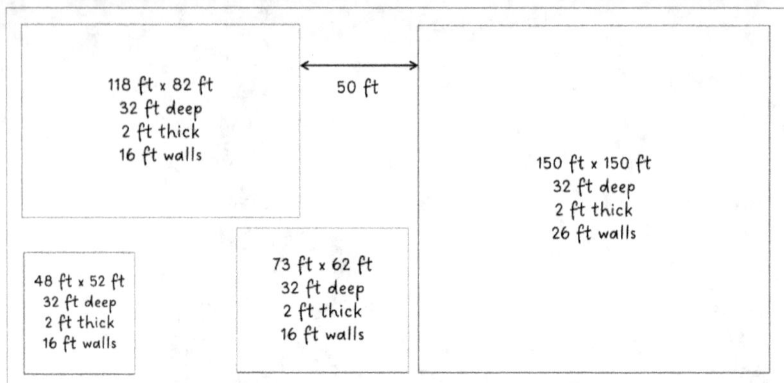

Sketch